SUBSTITUTE CHILD

JANE ELLYSON

PRAISE FOR SUBSTITUTE CHILD

An exciting thriller/romance taking a young Australian on a whirlwind journey. Surprised that I enjoyed it even more than Over Byron Bay (which I loved).

Tracie Rodwell

Substitute Child is a fast-paced thriller-romance from its opening pages in Byron Bay, to London, Paris, Antibes, Monte Carlo and Rome.

Sèverine Horvat

CONTENTS

FAMILY TREES

BOURNES, HARMONS, WYATTS

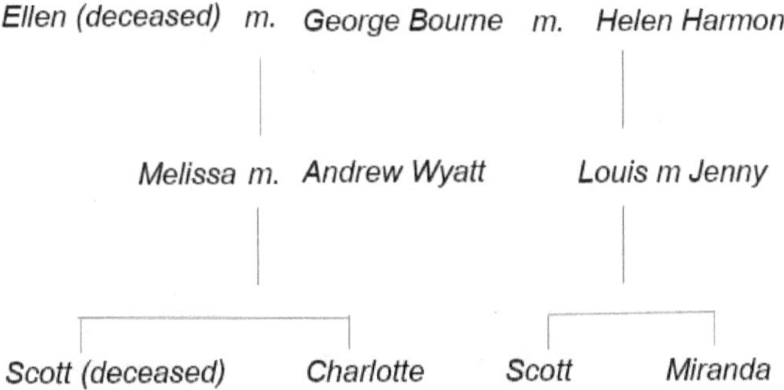

MAP OF FRANCE

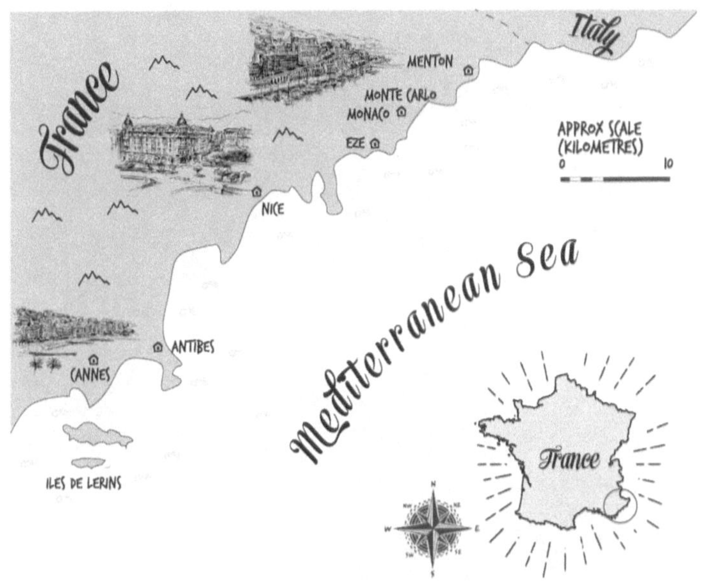

PROLOGUE

Together they gently released the bottle into the Pacific Ocean. It was a way for them to say goodbye to their son together. They watched in silence as it floated away with their messages of love. The sun was setting at the end of a beautiful day as they pulled up the anchor and sailed back to shore.

1

IDENTITY CRISIS

Scott Wyatt had been a constant presence in her life, which was surprising given that he'd died before she was born. Because of this, Charlotte Wyatt never quite felt she was an only child. In fact, some days she felt like the substitute child, a child born of grief, to replace the memory of a child who only lived a day.

No one ever called her *substitute child* to her face, but she heard it in the words not said. For example, when her mother would introduce her, she felt as though she could hear them thinking, 'Oh you're the child who came after Scott died'.

Her mother had been married before she met her father. Charlotte didn't know the details. There was definitely a back story to their relationship ...

2

BORED IN BRISBANE

Charlotte scowled as she reread her online diary.

March 15

Another crappy day.
So much to learn ... I thought I knew a lot. I know
nitsa.
This assignment has taken me twice as long as it
should.
Doubting my decision to drop fashion in favour of
the magic and mystery of digital media.
Everyone said there were no jobs in fashion design
in Australia and that all the interesting stuff was
happening in Asia and Europe.
Gotta get a job that will give me $$$ and get me a
ticket outta here.

Fed up being poor.
Fed up feeling like a failure.
Fed up with everything.

The diary was worth ten percent of her final marks in Media Issues. Don't suppose Professor Social was expecting this type of venting. Well, he did say I could write anything. So, voila! She was pleased to be able to use her high school French, even though this was probably another dead piece of knowledge she'd acquired in her *not spectacular* education to date.

Charlotte sighed as she stared at the Google search bar. She typed, 'What makes a story go viral?' In just over half a second there were nearly two million results. Ignoring the first page of results, she ran her eye down the articles appearing further down the search engine algorithm. It was her thing to see the articles that none of the other students in her class were likely to examine. A headline on Reddit caught her eye. She clicked on the link and read the post with increasing interest.

'Message in a bottle' from Byron Bay
picked up by French sailor

Found in the Mediterranean near Nice, France. A bottle from Byron Bay in Australia with a message to a child named Scott. Age of bottle unknown. No other names provided. The finder is searching for the owner through social media.

His request for help in finding Scott's parents has piqued the interest of millions in the Facebook and Twitter communities.

If you have any information about the letter writers, you can reach out to me at the following addresses.

I look forward to updating you on the unfolding story.

Mason Murray

'Mason Murray,' Charlotte whispered. 'Surely not?' She hadn't seen Mason for years, but he was a journalist wasn't he?'

She picked up her phone and dialled the third number on her speed dial.

'What's up, C?' chirped Miranda Harmon.

'That marvellous Mason, that friend of your brother you hankered after at school ... where he'd end up?'

'Mason Murray?'

'Yeah.'

'Last I heard he was training to be a journo.'

'D'you know where?'

'Nope.'

'Where's your brother? You could ask him.'

'He's on a yacht somewhere in the Caribbean. Only gets

internet access when he comes into port. I'll try to WhatsApp him and let you know.'

'Brilliant. Ta.'

'You gonna tell me why? Surely you don't have the hots for him too?'

'No, no, noooo,' Charlotte squealed, suppressing laughter. 'Just saw an article written by a Mason Murray in the British press. Wanted to know if it was your Mason Murray.'

'He's not *my Mason Murray*. If he's in the UK, that's a long way from home. But then he was always adventurous.'

'As well as handsome?'

'Too right. Blessed with many qualities.'

Charlotte smiled, said 'ta ta' and rang off. She sent a copy of the announcement to the printer, scooped it up and walked out to the kitchen where her parents were having their morning coffee.

'How's the assignment going, Purple Head?' her father said as she pulled up a chair to join them.

'Dad, how many times do I have to tell you that my hair is *not purple*. These highlights have *motions of mauve*,' she said with musical emphasis.

'I see,' he smiled. '*Motions of mauve*. I'll write that down. You know, in case anybody asks.'

Exasperated, Charlotte continued, ignoring her father's last comment, 'Might have found an interesting viral story with roots in Byron Bay for my assignment.'

'Really. Do tell.'

'Some guy in France found a bottle that's floated all the way from Byron Bay.'

Her father blinked and looked at her mother. Neither spoke, but her mother's forehead crinkled and the old scar like a spider's web, fluttered on her cheek. 'Seems the bottle was sent shortly after the death of a boy called Scott and ...'

A knock on the front door interrupted the conversation. As neither of her parents moved, Charlotte stood up and opened the door. She didn't recognise the smartly dressed woman with the microphone but quickly identified the commercial logo of the local television station.

'Hello. Good morning. We understand that the parents of Scott Wyatt live here?' It wasn't really a question, so Charlotte didn't feel compelled to respond. 'Can we have a few words with them ... about the bottle with the eulogy inside.' A cameraman who had previously been standing behind the woman stepped forward and zoomed in on Charlotte's face. She squirmed.

'Look, thanks for coming,' Charlotte gushed, quickly thinking on her feet. 'I understand why you're here and need to tell you we've already made an exclusive arrangement with another organisation.'

'You're kidding me. With who?'

'Mason Murray.'

'Mason Murray at *Hello*?'

'*Hello*?' Charlotte started before recovering. 'Yes, yes, that's him. I'm sorry you've had a wasted trip.'

The cameraman dropped the apparatus off his shoulder, fiddled with a cable and headed back to the van, followed by the woman with the microphone. Charlotte watched them leave and turned around to find her parents looking tentatively over her shoulder.

'I think we need to talk.'

'An exclusive contract? her father replied.

'I'm not sure I want to speak to anyone,' her mother said softly.

'Mum, the genie's out of the bottle. You're not gonna have a choice. What were you thinking when you let go of that bottle? Did it never occur to you that someone might find it?'

'I wasn't thinking. I was grieving. We were mourning and ... it was so hard to say goodbye. We just wanted to say goodbye together ...' her voice trailed off and she looked at her hands.

Numerous questions popped into Charlotte's head.

'Mum.' Her mother looked up. 'I'll manage this.' Melissa Wyatt said nothing and looked at her husband. He nodded.

'We're going for a walk.'

Charlotte imagined they had a lot to talk about.

3

———

INVITATION TO LONDON

She returned to her room and plopped into her desk chair, swivelling it from side to side impatiently. Her phone pinged and the message 'call me' flashed on the screen. She dialled her friend.

'Yo M, What's up?'

'Exciting news. I've heard from my bro. And he says that Mason is your man in London.'

'Ahhh, interesting. And how is he finding the Caribbean?'

'Gone or going. On his way to Spain sailing across the pond as he says. OMG. D'ya need anything else?'

'Nah – think that's it for now.'

'Righto. And do ya wanna tell me what this is about?'

'Err. It's a little bit of a long story ... about my *dead* brother.'

Silence.

'What?'

'Let's catch up later. Got things I've gotta do. Tricky conversation to have with the olds. See ya tonight at Brewskis. I'll tell you everything then'

'Too right. You've lots of explaining to do, C.'

Charlotte googled international clock and guessed Mason would be asleep in London. She dropped him a note with a link to the post.

Saw this piece with your name. Can you confirm this is you? Charlotte Wyatt.

Short. Sufficient. Send. She was pretty confident he'd remember her. Miranda and Scott's grandmother, Helen, was married to Charlotte's grandfather, so she'd seen a bit of them growing up. Scott would sometimes bring Mason along to family get-togethers.

Charlotte sighed as she stared at her screen. Absolutely no idea what I'm doing, she mused. As she stood up to walk to the kitchen her phone pinged. There was a WhatsApp message from Mason.

Call me.

Startled by the speed of response to her message, she pressed the call icon.

'Hello?'

'Hey, Mason, remember me?' I guess it's been six or so years since we last spoke.'

'Yeah of course. Who could forget those grand BBQs your grandparents would host.'

'Too right.' She caught her breath, thinking about his use of the word *grand*. Very British. 'To bring you up to speed. I'm studying digital media at QUT. And that's kinda the reason I got in touch with you. I saw your post about the bottle. It was my parents who polluted the environment by throwing it into the sea twenty years ago.'

'Blimey,' he responded. Charlotte grimaced at the odd colloquialism.

'Of course, they would've preferred no one knew about it and they didn't expect it to be found, or for themselves to be identified as the authors. And of course, it goes without saying that they didn't expect the back story to be a subject of public interest. It's a bit much for them – but it is what it is.'

'You're right. This story is a cracker. And the fact that it comes from Byron Bay is brilliant for me.' He paused. 'Anyway. Tell me what you need.'

'We just had a visit from reporters from the local TV station, who I fobbed off. I took an educated guess that you'd written the story so I told them you had the exclusive as a way of controlling this, on the understanding that whatever you write will be sensitive and respectful to their loss.'

A pause on the other end of the line.

'Understood. Of course. Perfectly reasonable request. This story has huge human-interest and circulation boosting power which is why my boss is so interested. Let me chat to a few people, but I'm quietly confident that I might be able to wangle you a free ticket to London to be interviewed and photographed for the story in place of your parents . Would you be open to that?'

'Would I be open to accepting a free ticket to London? Are you kidding me?'

'Give me another ten hours or so. It's just after midnight here. I'll pitch the idea to my boss first thing tomorrow and let you know what she says. What's the best way to contact you?'

They exchanged details and said goodbye. Charlotte heard the front door close. She walked slowly back to the kitchen, thinking through her next conversation with her parents.

4

PARENTAL OBJECTIONS

'So, I've just been in touch with Mason Murray, you remember Mason? He's Scott Harmon's mate. Well he seems to think he may be able to wrangle a free ticket for someone in our family to fly to London for an interview. Would that be OK?'

'No,' replied her father. 'Isn't that what the Internet is for? Surely you can give him what he needs by email? You don't need to go there yourself,' he said firmly, said guessing that the *someone* had already been identified by his wily daughter as herself. 'What about your studies? I can't see how this would be a sensible thing to do. You can't afford to drop out of your studies *again*.'

Ouch. That hurt.

'You're too young, Charlotte,' her mother chipped in. 'You've never travelled anywhere on your own overseas.'

'Ahem, Mum. Can you remind me how old you were when you left Bangalow for Boston?'

Her mother raised her eyebrows. 'Twenty,' she replied sheepishly.

'Twenty. If only I was twenty. Oh wait. I'll be twenty in eight months.'

'So why don't you wait until then?'

Charlotte realised she should have better anticipated their objections.

'The story is happening now. I know it's not 'news' but no one will care about this in six months' time. Let's just see what Mason comes back with. This is huge. An opportunity for the story to be told by a friend. And a way to ensure the story is told the way we want. And I may well end up with a brilliant assignment for uni. All I ask is that you think about it. Just think about it.'

Charlotte returned to her room before they could respond, recognising her parents needed time alone again to talk, while she thought through her arguments for overcoming their concerns. She opened her online learning journal and continued typing.

15 March. Opportunities and Objections

Opportunities

Be a part of an exciting story. OMG
Get to London to communicate properly about the
bottle from Byron Bay
Get great content for my assignment and achieve
superior marks
Have fun. LOL
See the sites of London.
Go shopping for clothes. Yes.
Have fun. (Point needs to be made twice)
Yikes

Likely Parental Objections

1. You're studying – can't afford to give up or fail this subject having dropped out of fashion.

Action: Talk to Prof and get time off sorted. Highlight that I'll only be going for a week.

2. You don't have any cash. True.

Action: Talk to Grandpa.

3. You'll be mugged, raped, swindled, ruined …etc.

Action: Reassure them that I will be with Mason at all times. Remind them that he's a heroic lifesaver and will surely save me from any trouble I may encounter.

5

____

WINNING THE ARGUMENT

Charlotte grabbed her phone the following morning at 5:00am to check her messages. Mason's email was at the top.

Yo, Charlotte. Have I got news for you? Not only am I getting you a free ticket to London, but you'll also be going to Paris. Seems we've negotiated a partnership deal with Paris-Match who are also very keen to meet you. They've something particular in mind that they've not shared with us yet, but I know it will involve fashion. You're still interested in fashion, aren't you?

You're kidding me? I love beautiful fabrics and fashion. Let's talk.

Mason called her immediately.

'Good. We've been throwing around some ideas on how to pitch this story. Hana at *Paris Match* is keen to get photos of you, the Aussie student and sister of Scott, meeting Jacques, the undoubtedly handsome and intrepid sailor who found the bottle. They're investigating the possibility of flying him to Paris. Be warned – they'll most likely stage the photos so it looks like there's a love interest. It helps sell magazines.' Charlotte suppressed a giggle.

'Don't think I'll share that bit with Mum. She's anxious enough.'

'Understood,' Mason laughed. 'OK. So, here's the deal. *Hello* and *Paris-Match* will share your costs in flying you to London, in economy of course. You can stay at my flat for a few nights, then we'll take the train to Paris, staying in an undoubtedly not very impressive hotel on the Right Bank for a night or two, and then back to London for your journey home to Australia. Estimated time between departure and arrival home no more than ten days. I know it's a long way for such a short trip and that you're likely to not quite get over the jet lag, but what do you reckon? Do you think it's a goer?'

'Leave it with me. I've got things to do to prepare for Mum's inevitable objections but I'll get back to you soon. If I possibly can, I'll be there with bells on. Tell your boss it's looking good and keep your fingers crossed for me.'

'Too right. Talk soon.'

Charlotte was quivering with excitement as she hung up. She quickly sent an email to her professor of Digital Media Studies, who was conveniently named Peter Social, highlighting the value of this opportunity to undertake primary research and asking to be excused from tutorials for a week. With the email sent she climbed back into bed but couldn't sleep. Her head was buzzing with the opportunity this trip provided to get out of Brisbane.

She checked her email box three hours later and was

concerned to see an ominously headed email saying *Call me*. Charlotte phoned the professor and quickly addressed all the points of concern. She was particularly pleased with his final comment.

'It would be a sad day if we in Digital Studies couldn't accommodate a student working on the other side of the world. We'd be failing to achieve one of our principle objectives. So best of luck and don't forget to update your reflective journal at the end of each day. I'm looking forward to reading it already.'

Next, Charlotte called her grandfather. He was a loving ally and she was confident of his support. She explained the opportunity and had a big ask. As expected, he said *'Of course.'* Possessing all the relevant information and with her key supporters onside she had a shower and put on her favourite dress, a vintage style shift, along with a tiny cardigan with sparkles on the sleeves she'd bought at the Byron Bay markets. Feeling empowered, she joined her parents for breakfast.

'Everything is all set for me to go to London.'

'Wait just one moment there, Purple Head. I think you're getting ahead of yourself.'

'Mason told me this morning that not only am I going to London but also to Paris. The trip has extended a little since yesterday. I'll probably be gone for a week, but definitely no more than ten days.'

'You can't go for a week. You don't have enough money.'

'Mum, my costs are tiny. Flights to London and accommodation in Paris are paid for *a grace a Hello* and *Paris-Match* who want me for a fashion shoot as well as a story.' Charlotte thought this was the perfect time to show off her high school French. 'And I've already spoken to Grandpa who has kindly given me my birthday gift in advance.'

Melissa Wyatt tutted out loud, cranky at her father's mutinous behaviour.

'I've also spoken with my prof, who is excited about this opportunity for me and is already looking forward to reading my final assignment and reflective journal. I'm sure I'll get a seven in this subject, that is, if you let me go. Any other objections?'

Her parents looked at each other tentatively.

'I don't want you to go honey. Can you leave it at that?'

'No, Mum. What are you afraid of?'

'What if you fall in love with a charming Frenchman and never come home?'

Melissa's father started laughing and her mother shook her head.

'Don't,' she snapped at him.

He put his arm around her and pulled her close.

'What about safety? You might be mugged,' her mother continued.

'Mum, I'll be with Mason all the time. In the unlikely event of being mugged we'll go to the police. Isn't that what you'd do?' Silence. 'Mum,' Charlotte offered gently. 'What are you really afraid of?' Silence again.

'I don't want to let you go. I couldn't stand to lose you.'

And once again the unsaid reference to Scott was there.

'I promise I'll be careful. I'll be back in Brisbane on the 27th of March. I promise.' Her father nodded while her mother buried her head in his shoulder.

6

———

LEAVING ON A JET PLANE

Flights were confirmed and Melissa stuffed and then emptied her bag. Her father reminded her that it would be cold in London and gave her his credit card with permission to pick up one or two warm items *only* on arrival. She hugged him and shrieked with excitement.

Twelve hours later she was seated in row 56C on her way to London via Singapore with British Airways. Being seated close to the bathroom, she thought she was well positioned until she realised she'd always get her meal last and there'd be a regular queue of people beside her seat waiting to visit the amenities. She sighed, not really caring, and did a last check of her messages before shutting down her electronic devices. There was a message from Miranda.

*Have a fab time ... well, not *too* fab a time with Mason.*
Tee hee. Message often.

She smiled and settled down to watch three movies before they arrived in Singapore, She loved the shops at the airport and nearly missed the call to reboard as she was trying on a dress that definitely didn't qualify as a 'warm item' as stipulated by her father. Once back on board she watched another three movies before finally falling into a deep sleep when the plane was less than four hours from landing at London Heathrow.

It was hard to wake up and get out of the seat. Everyone was emptying the overhead bins and putting on their coats. It was cold and suddenly she felt nervous. What would she do if Mason wasn't there to meet her? Weariness and nerves were playing games with her confidence. There was an endless line of people waiting in the *Others* queues to be processed at immigration. Finally, she made it to the front of the queue. The surly border agent with an enormous grey moustache regarded her with disinterest.

'Passport,' he said flatly. 'First visit to London?' Charlotte nodded. 'Purpose of visit?'

'A story,' Charlotte blurted out without thought.

'A story?'

'Yes, a long story, and you probably wouldn't believe it.'

'Are you a journalist?'

'No.'

'A writer'

'Well, no.'

'What are you then?'

'To be honest I don't know what I am. I mean. I'm a student. I'm a sister. Well, I would've been a sister if my brother had lived.'

'What?'

'I'm here to help write a story about my brother with *Hello*. Do you know the magazine *Hello*?' Charlotte was suddenly, able to form coherent sentences.

'Yes, I know that magazine. And how long will you be in Britain?'

'Just three days'

'And how will you support yourself while you're here?'

'I have money from my grandfather, and my Dad's credit card, but only for emergencies and essential clothing, of course.' A slight smile breached the agent's face. 'And I'll be staying with a friend.' He stamped her passport and yelled out *'Next'*. Relieved, Charlotte hurried through to the baggage area, collecting her things, and then out into the Arrivals hall.

'G'day', Mason called out from behind the metal barrier. 'Welcome to London.' A few people looked at them and smiled. 'How was the flight?'

'Awesome. Six films and three glasses of wine. All things I would've been in big trouble for at home.'

'And did you get plenty of sleep?'

'Well ... a little. I'll be OK.'

'Good. We have so much to do and so little time. First stop my flat to drop off your things, then shower followed by essential liquids, then into our offices to meet my boss, Jane. There'll be lots of questions and photos and that's just for starters. But firstly, can I suggest you let your parents know you've arrived safely. Here.' Murray passed her his phone.

Charlotte thumbed a quick message.

Arrived safely. Now here with Mason. Plenty of sleep. Hugs Purple Head

It was mostly true.

'Thanks. That was important. Can we get a Sim card for my phone today?'

'Of course. And I've been instructed by your mother to get your phone set up with tracking so I always know where you are.'

Charlotte raised her eyebrows while Mason scooped up her bag. His phone started ringing seconds later.

'I think this is for you.'

Charlotte looked at the number.

'Hi Dad.'

'Hey Princess. Thanks for the message. I'll be quick. Stick with Mason at all times and keep that credit card closer. Don't go out on your own. Have a safe time and we look forward to hearing all about it when you're home on 27 March.'

'Got it Dad. And if it's OK, I plan to have a good time while I'm here. Gotta go. Love to Mum.'

She handed the phone back to Mason and looked around her as they shuffled down to *the tube*. The airport was buzzing with noise and activity. Everyone was going somewhere. Charlotte loved the diversity of the people; so many colours, languages and accents. There were people on business, with their families or their sport's team and the range of clothing styles was exciting. She was impressed by Mason's long grey woollen coat, that accentuated his tall frame and russet curls. The train pulled in and they grabbed two seats together. The Piccadilly Line train hurtled and rattled into the city in the dark of the early morning.

Mason's flat was ten-minute walk from West Kensington station. It was kind of charming and kind of creepy at the same time. It was occupied by five blokes with not a high attention to hygiene, with the wallpaper in the bathroom peeling off from the damp. Charlotte didn't care and slumped onto the sofa.

'No time for slouching. Shower, then cup of tea, then meeting.'

With Mason bossing her around it felt like she was still at home. No, it didn't, she scolded herself as she entered the damp dungeon for a wash.

HELLO, HELLO

'Brilliant. She's here,' Jane Sweet screeched, embracing Charlotte as if she was a long-lost friend. Charlotte was momentarily taken aback.

'Welcome to London. We're so thrilled to have you here. Thanks for coming.'

'Thanks for inviting me,' Charlotte replied, smiling broadly while noting the gorgeous, Picasso-inspired print maxi dress swishing around Jane's tiny frame.

'This story has such potential. Girl from small country town in Australia comes to Europe to collect the bottle with messages for her dead brother. A great human-interest story. I hope you're prepared for a bit of fame and attention from the paparazzi. You're rather photogenic.'

She squirmed at the compliment. 'Happy to be the face of the Wyatt family as long as we can keep my parents, and particularly my mother, out of the media spotlight.'

'Understood. We know this is a sensitive story. We'll do our best. So, first, impressions of London?'

'Wonderful, colourful, cold and damp.'

'Well, it is autumn. You'll soon learn to never to go out without a brolly.'

Charlotte smiled. 'Understood.'

'This morning we'll take photos and this afternoon we'll plan the pieces Mason will write to ensure the story gets maximum visibility.' Charlotte nodded tentatively. 'You'll get to see the sights. Big Ben, Trafalgar Square, St Paul's, the Tower of London. Mason will take you, with a cameraman of course. We could run a story, *Impressions from an Aussie's first day in London*.'

'OK,' Charlotte replied hesitatingly. 'What's your plan for the story of the bottle and my brother?'

Mason outlined the structure he had in mind. Jane nodded. 'We'll need to see what ideas *Paris-Match* has, but I'll make sure we're clear on the boundaries of the story in order to protect your parents' privacy. Why don't you two young folk go out now and see the sights. Charlotte, do you want to pick up a few pieces of more weather-appropriate wear from our wardrobe department? I'm sure we have a lot of new season samples in your size. Mick will take a few photos of you in your new threads. Mason, don't forget to get back here before our call with Hana at 4:00.' Mason saluted Jane and directed Charlotte to the wardrobe room. Charlotte felt like she was in Aladdin's cave. She selected a white, cable-weave jumper, traditional black woollen coat, a pair of Doc Martens, thick socks and a few scarves of assorted colours. Mason threw her a beanie with a Union Jack. She grimaced.

'Now we're ready,' he declared. 'Look out London. Charlotte Wyatt has arrived.'

It was all a bit of a blur by early afternoon, but Charlotte remembered driving past Hyde Park, Buckingham Palace, Trafalgar Square, The Strand and St Paul's, although not necessarily in that order. She posed for pictures near Tower Bridge, occasionally wearing that silly hat before she was suddenly gripped by intense, jet-lag induced hunger pains and they stopped for large portions of fish and chips. With Charlotte sated and feeling increasingly sleepy, they returned to *Hello*'s offices for the call with *Paris-Match*. They all snuggled around the phone in a conference room which was not much bigger than one of the red telephone boxes they'd walked past earlier.

'Oui, 'allo Charlotte,' crooned Hana, in the sexiest voice Charlotte had ever heard.

'Bonjour Hana. Je suis très heureux de vous rencontrer.' Jane and Mason raised their eyebrows. Where did that broad Australian accent disappear to?

'Vous parlez Français? Et vous avez un accent merveilleux.'

'Vous êtes trop gentil.'

'Nous devrions parler Anglais. We must speak English.'

'Of course.'

'So ... you catch the early train to Paris on Wednesday and come here to *Paris-Match*. We can then take some photos both in our studio and at a few other locations. And of course, we talk about the story. Charlotte, I hope to have your sailor and your bottle here for you by the time you arrive. He is currently on the ship so communication is a little tricky. Do you have any questions?'

'Pas pour la moment,' Charlotte replied.

'Bien. I look forward to meeting you both on Wednesday morning.'

'We do too.'

They rang off and walked back out into the main office.

Charlotte yawned and looked out the window. It was dark.

'Ready to go back to my flat, Miss Wyatt?'

'Brilliant,' Charlotte replied, imitating the enthusiastic mantra of Jane.

'So, tomorrow, you two.' They both looked at Jane. 'Great to get more photos. Charlotte, is there anywhere you particularly want to see?'

'Well, I am rather interested in fashion and shopping.'

'Say no more.' Jane picked up her notepad and began scribbling furiously. 'Mason.'

'Yep?'

'Take this list tomorrow and show Charlotte why London is one of the top fashion cities in the world.' Mason looked at the list, smiled and then popped it into his top pocket.

'Will do.'

Charlotte and Mason arrived back at his flat around six that evening, after a short stop to pick up a SIM card. After it was successfully installed two messages were sent:

Message 1: *Hi Mum & Dad. Great first day in London. Mason is looking after me. Suspect we'll have an early night. Love PH*

Message 2: *Hey Miranda. I'm here. OMG #SoExcited Getting ready to go out for a tandoori and to have a look around even though it is ****** cold. More soon. C*

'Phew. Done.' Charlotte smiled at Mason.

'Nope, not yet. One more thing. Your mum is concerned for your safety.'

'Do ya wanna tell me something I don't know?'

Ignoring her attitude, he continued. 'I use the Strava App for cycling. It lets me show everyone where I am on the road. Let me put it on your phone, too. It's just a peace of mind thing. If you get lost, I should be able to find you quickly.'

'If you insist,' she replied, passing her phone back to him.

''Allo, 'allo, 'allo. Who's this?' A chubby, Englishman in a suit announced his arrival as he walked into the kitchen.

'Tom, this is Charlotte. Charlotte, Tom. She's a friend from Australia helping me with a story. She'll be couch surfing for a couple of nights.'

'If the sofa's too uncomfortable, Charlotte, there's plenty of room in my bedroom.'

'Thank you, Tom, but that won't be necessary,' Mason said barely disguising his annoyance as he flicked his curly fringe out of his eyes and pushed his glasses up his nose.

'Can't blame a bloke for trying. Not often we get a beauty in our bachelor pad.' Voices in the hallway announced the arrival of more residents. Mason introduced Scottish Simon, Welsh Will and Kev from New Zealand. Introductions over, Mason took Charlotte into his bedroom where it was easier to talk.

'Take a seat and have a look at this list of fashion-related locations Jane's suggested for tomorrow. I'm going to grab a shower before Waterhog Will drains the tank. Then we can plan our itinerary.'

'Will do,' Charlotte replied, pulling off her shoes and plopping down on his bed. Most of the places were unfamiliar to her, so she rearranged the pillows, lay down and started googling each one on her phone. Reading the small print was hard work and she suddenly felt tired. I'm just going to close my eyes for two minutes, she said to herself. Ten minutes later Mason returned from the shower to see Charlotte sound asleep.

'Well, looks like we'll be having tandoori tomorrow night, Miss Wyatt.' He pulled the blankets over her and turned off the light.

8

ABOUT LAST NIGHT

Charlotte woke up with a start at 5:00am. Momentarily disoriented by the unfamiliar surroundings, she tried to adjust her eyes to the dark. It was hard. A tiny light in the corner revealed a phone being recharged. She rolled on her back and was suddenly aware that someone else was on the bed. Turning ever so slowly she discovered Mason, sound asleep beside her, still fully-dressed. She was wide awake now, but dared not move in case she disturbed him. There was movement in the hallway. A toilet flushed and a kettle was being filled in the kitchen. One of the other inhabitants was getting ready for the day. Charlotte rolled back on her side and reached over to the floor, feeling around for her phone. Delighted at finding it, she switched it on.

Message 1: *Morning Princess. Pleased you went to bed early after the long flight. Keep close to Mason and keep in touch. Hugs, Mum and Dad*

Message 2: *I wanna know what you did last night. Waiting! Miranda*

Charlotte groaned and inadvertently woke Mason.

'Sorry,' she whispered.

'No worries,' he replied. 'Everyone well at home?'

Charlotte nodded and sat up on the bed. 'Can I get you a cup of something?'

'Yes please. Tea. With milk.'

Troublesome Tom was in the kitchen eating toast and marmalade when Charlotte shuffled in.

'Morning,' he offered with an irritating smirk.

'Morning,' she replied.

'How was the sofa?' he asked.

'We both know that I didn't sleep on the sofa. I slept in Mason's bed. We both slept very well, before you ask.'

'If that's your story it's fine with me.' He took a noisy slurp of his tea before finishing off his toast. Charlotte made a fresh pot and returned to Mason's room.

'I have either damaged or enhanced your reputation in Tom's eyes this morning,' she said, passing him a steaming mug.

'Pfft. Don't give a toss what he thinks. However, this will need to be our little secret. Would hate it if your mum knew.'

'Agreed.'

'How you feeling?'

'Brilliant and ready to hit the High Street.'

'Let's go.'

Mick was waiting for them downstairs in the dark with an umbrella.

'Morning. Did you both have a nice evening?'

'It was fairly uneventful,' Mason replied crinkling his nose.

'Yep. We went to bed early,' Charlotte chipped in, laughing. Mason smiled while Mick shook his head, confused.

'Where am I taking you first?'

'Given that most shops aren't open yet, I think we should do some window shopping. Head for Oxford Circus and we'll get out near Carnaby Street. That's a great place to take a few memorable snaps.'

'Roger that. Follow me. Our driver is waiting in the van around the corner.'

It was quiet on Carnaby Street, except for a song playing softly on an outdoor speaker that was vaguely familiar to Charlotte. She remembered last hearing it at her grandmother Helen's place in Byron Bay. Helen Harmon, technically speaking, wasn't her grandmother. She'd married her grandfather George Bourne, not long after the accident that had resulted in her brother's death. Helen had lived in Byron Bay until she met Charlotte's grandfather, who lived nearby, just out of Bangalow. Helen's house at Byron Bay was popular with family members and friends, particularly during summer as it was 500 metres from the beach. It was where Charlotte had occasionally met Helen's grandson Scott Harmon and his best friend Mason Murray. In fact, it was Scott who used to sing this song, calling her *Charlie Girl*. As she listened, Charlotte realised that the singer wasn't actually saying, *Hey there Charlie Girl*, but *Hey there Georgy Girl*. Typical, Charlotte thought to herself. Most things Scott

Harmon said and did annoyed her. Like the secret relationship he had with her mother. Why did he call her 'mermaid'? That was never explained.

'Charlotte. Earth to Charlotte?' Mason enquired. 'You OK to pose under the *Welcome to Carnaby Street* archway?'

'You bet,' she responded, pleased to break from her thoughts. She lifted her scarf in the air between her hands and yelled out,

'I'm not Charlie Girl. Look out London!'

Reflective Journal: London, Tuesday, 20 March

I'm stuffed. Totally stuffed – but in such a good way.
Had the most brilliant day.
We started at Carnaby Street. Beautiful street fronts
and cute shops.
Was in fabric heaven in Liberty.

Then cruised down Oxford Street.
Red buses. Black taxis.
Spent more time checking out the people than the
shops – well, to start with anyway.
The hair. The shoes. The attitude. Looooove it.
Confident people – always the worker bees,
Overwhelmed people – the touristees.

Cruised down to Piccadilly Circus
And through Leicester Square,
Thousands of people and

Buskers Everywhere.

Then took the tube to Camden Lock.
Much more my kinda place.
Black stuff.
Big Boots.
Markets galore,
Tattoo invitations. Tempted. Mum would kill me –
I'm sure.

Love the sizzling smells
And the general chill-out factor.
Walked with growing attitude,
While listening to a rapper.

Mick took snaps of me
on a bridge,
on a boat
and against a brick wall.

'Hey check out the model'
I heard someone call

'Who, me?'
I whispered.

Charlotte stopped typing and looked at the words she
had written.
Who me? indeed.

She continued typing.

With a million snaps secured
We said *Hoo Roo Mick*
And took the tube south
To visit the Vic
(Well, the Victoria and Albert museum).

Inspired by fashion through the ages
Scribbling furiously pages on pages

Can't believe how time flies soaking up the art
Until chased out the door at five and into the wintery
dark.

Charlotte paused and pondered before continuing.

We walked back to West Kensington and picked up
tandoori for tea
Which apparently is a local speciality.

Terrible Tom was out for the night
Humungous relief – the other lads were a delight.

Hard to get new threads into my bag
Evidence of damage done to Dad's credit card

Must tell him ... soon

Charlotte suddenly remembered she hadn't responded
to the messages from her parents or Miranda.

Message 1: *Hi Mum and Dad. Continued research for my
assignment and Mason's article. Managed to slip in sightseeing such as trip to fabulous Victoria and Albert*

Museum. Very educational. Will have another early night to bed in preparation for journey to Paris tomorrow. Hugs Purple Head.

Message 2: *Hey M, Having awesome time in London. Lots of sightseeing and me posing for pics in front of famous places. Nearly got a tattoo. Eyebrow raise from Mason. Not impressed. He lives in squidgy flat with mostly nice others – except for Tosser Tom. I do like your Mason. More soon. C*

There were a few half-truths, information not provided and questions not responded to. They could wait.

9

ST PANCRAS TO PARIS

Reflective journal – Day 4 of European adventure

Groan.
Writing this on the train as we pull out of St Pancras.
Needed the alarm to get off the sofa this morning in
order to make the 5:40 train.
Why oh why did I go to bed at eleven?
Mason being super nice providing cups of tea and
moral encouragement.
He really is sweet although not my type of course.

'Stop writing and look out the window, Miss Wyatt.'
'It's so dark and there's nothing to see. And stop call me
Miss Wyatt.'
A slight smile flickered across Mason's lips and his green

eyes crinkled. 'One day you'll be so famous that I'll be lucky to address you as anything else.'

Charlotte wanted to respond with something sarcastic but caught herself. Maybe the story would go crazy and she *would* be famous. What would that be like? She pulled a notepad out of her backpack and turned to a new page.

'Time for you to help me with my assignment question. First question. What are the characteristics of a story that goes viral on the internet?'

'Easy. Three things. Beauty, royalty and/or celebrity and a story that captures people's imagination. You have two of these things already.' Charlotte blushed and kept her eyes firmly focussed on her notepad. Mason continued. 'You've a story which I think we'll title *Beauty and the Bottle* which will make an emotional connection with many people. It has elements of love, loss and a journey across time. And with these components combined, the story should spread widely and you'll become a celebrity. Sans doubt.'

Charlotte grimaced. 'And how will we know when we've achieved viral status?'

'Again easy. Obviously, there's magazine sales which of course may or may not be related to a single photo or article. However, through our social media channels across Facebook, Twitter, Instagram, YouTube and Pinterest we'll be able to see the level of engagement with the photos, videos and stories. We'll share our data with *Paris-Match* and leverage traditional media as well. We can count newspaper articles and TV interviews as two of many indicators. The fact that there are so many angles, again increases the probability of success. I'm optimistic, and selfishly have to admit that this story will be great for my career.'

Charlotte raised her eyebrows and smiled. 'Pleased to be able to help.'

'Hey look,' he interrupted, 'we're about to go into the tunnel under the English Channel.'

Charlotte felt disappointed that there was little to see as they sped underground. It didn't feel any different to travelling on land. She shrugged her shoulders, leaned against the freezing cold window and fell asleep, thinking about what life would be like once her parent's story was told.

It was half past nine as the Eurostar came to a halt at Gare du Nord and Mason gently shook her. She dragged her heavy case along behind him and momentarily regretted buying the funky suede boots at Camden Market.

'It's half an hour by train to Anatole-France or forty-five minutes by taxi. Option one is cheaper and faster, but getting a ticket is a drag.'

'Let's take the train. I'll go get the tickets. You mind the luggage.'

Mason nodded and Charlotte scooted off on her own. There were no staffed ticket offices that she could see, and a queue of over twenty people for a single ticket machine. She joined the line and waited patiently with the other tourists as they slowly shuffled forward.

'Boring, eh?' came a voice from behind. Charlotte turned to see a young couple with backpacks.

'Where you from?' the girl wearing denim dungarees asked in perfect English.

'Australia.'

'Kangaroo country.'

'Kind of, well, not exactly.' Charlotte replied while trying to get her foggy brain to give a more coherent answer.

'We are you going this morning?'

'*Paris-Match*'s office at Anatole-France.'

'Thought you could be a model. We've already bought tickets for that line. Would you like to buy them from us rather than waiting in the queue?'

Charlotte could see that the queue had now stopped moving. She looked at her watch and then back at the young couple.

'Sure. That'd be great. How much to I owe you for two tickets?

'Twenty euros will do it.'

Charlotte fumbled around in her wallet looking for a twenty euro note as she was not yet familiar with the currency. 'Ah ha. Here you go.'

'And there you go. Don't forget to change at Reaumur-Sebastopol.'

'Brilliant, thank you.' She waved goodbye and returned to Mason who was on the phone.'

'Yep, so we should be there shortly. Charlotte is just back with our tickets. See you soon Hana.'

'Got them.' Charlotte handed a ticket to Mason.

'How much did they cost?'

'Twenty euros.'

'Hmm. That's steep. Might've been cheaper to get a taxi. Oh well. Here you go.'

Charlotte went to put the notes Mason had passed her into her wallet and noticed that several notes were missing. Momentarily confused, she counted her money and confirmed her worst suspicions.

'Those thieving bastards. How'd they do it? And they got Dad's credit card. And I don't believe for a nano-second that these tickets are valid.'

Curses merged into tears. Charlotte felt stupid for having trusted these strangers. Maybe her mother was right, and she was too young to travel on her own. Her parents would be upset and she hated the thought of telling them. Mason put his arm around her and pulled her close. She took a deep breath. She was being silly. At least she wasn't alone. She had Mason. Marvellous Mason. Miranda's Mason. Feeling guilty, she wriggled out of his embrace and wiped the tears off her cheeks.

'Let's go report this. If we can stop someone else getting ripped off then this crappy experience won't be a total loss.'

They dragged their bags to the Commissariat de Police on rue De Mauberge. Feeling more in control, Charlotte explained in French what had happened. The gendarmes were sympathetic and not surprised by the deception suffered by the young Australian. This was not the first complaint of this kind they'd received. After viewing a few minutes of video footage from inside the station, Charlotte was able to identify the rogue backpackers who were quickly picked up and brought in, protesting their innocence. When they saw Charlotte and the video, they reluctantly accepted their fate and returned her money and credit card. She was elated. Victory. And as an added bonus, they were given a lift in a police car to *Paris-Match*'s offices by way of thank you. Charlotte was smiling like a Cheshire cat when her phone pinged with a WhatsApp message. It was her father.

First impressions of Paris?

Charlotte smiled and hesitated before responding.

Largely uneventful trip. Can you believe I fell asleep in the tunnel?

Had a fab and fast taxi ride to Paris-Match's office. About to start work. More later.

Her father sent back a smiley emoji. (• ˇ‿ˇ •) Charlotte was suddenly aware she hadn't received a message from Miranda. Odd. She typed a short note.

Just arrived in gay Paris. Lots to tell you M. More later. Hope all good 4 u? C

10

PARIS-MATCH

'Bienvenue,' Hana cooed as she kissed them on both cheeks. 'An uneventful journey I hope?' Mason looked at Charlotte and hesitated before responding.

'The usual. We slept most of the way on the train.'

'Good. You will need your rest as we have a busy schedule for you both. But first, we take coffee.'

'Parfait,' Charlotte replied. 'A little something to wake me up would be great.' Mason winked at her as they followed Hana to a nearby café. After several espressos and croissants, the new plan was described. Things hadn't quite worked out as intended. Hana had hoped to bring Jacques, the sailor who had found the bottle, to Paris, but it was not possible as he needed to stay with the yacht.

'So, we have decided to send you both to the south of France to meet with Jacques on his ship. You will fly to Nice and be collected by a reporter from *Nice-Matin* who will take you to your hotel in Antibes, where you'll drop off your bags, and then down to the port where there will be a series of photo shoots with Jacques, Charlotte and the 'magic bottle' before a few more photos around the old town. Does that sound reasonable?'

'Absolument,' Charlotte replied.

'And of course, *Paris-Match* will pick up the costs of the flights and one night's accommodation in Antibes.

'Ici in Paris,' Hana went on with an adorable French/English melange, 'we will continue with the theme of a young Australian girl in Paris for the first time. I think it would be fun to do a transformation, if that would be OK with Charlotte?'

'Bien sûr, this trip is an adventure pour moi,' Charlotte said, modelling Hana's mix of French and English. 'I need to shake off the old me and try new things. So oui, oui, oui, I want to try new looks, visit new places, sample French foods and live a little dangerously.'

'Parfait. I think that your peasant look is charming and I would like to shoot you like this. Then we try something *une peu classique* and more in line with *les look* de *Paris-Match*.' Charlotte smiled and raised her eyebrows at Mason, who was clearly bemused. 'And your hair? We can try something a little different here too? Jean,' Hana called out to an assistant. 'Take Charlotte to makeup and wardrobe. We will be doing a *two-face* special. You know what I want.'

'Viens,' Jean signalled to Charlotte while winking at Hana.

'Show me some of your vintage clothes.' Charlotte opened her suitcase and Jean quickly sorted through her clothes.

'This, this and this. Parfait. Mireille?'

'Oui,' replied the makeup artist.

'I want a look which is a little bohemian and very whimsical.'

Charlotte picked up the clothes Jean had selected and

sat in the chair offered by Mireille, who started dabbling her face with brushes. Still feeling a little jet-lagged, Charlotte looked around the room at the gorgeous clothes and then at her reflection in the mirror. Is that really you, Charlotte Wyatt, sitting in that chair like a princess? she asked herself while nodding off to sleep. No, not a princess. I'm Cinderella and at any moment I'm going to wake up on a beach with a bottle.

Charlotte sneezed and woke up. Jean had been tickling her with a feather.

'Sleeping Beauty tomorrow. Today we must work.'

Charlotte looked in the mirror and barely recognised herself.

'La cabine is there,' Jean pointed to the change room while switching a button on a remote device to flood the room with the sound of a guitar. It was beautiful and vaguely familiar. Charlotte put on her favourite blue cotton gypsy blouse, combined with a three -tiered skirt and new suede boots and suddenly felt more herself. She was humming as she walked to the stage set, where there were baskets of flowers in a wheelbarrow and fruit in a basket, and started swaying to the music. She smiled when she heard John Denver belt out the lyrics to *Leaving On a Jet Plane*. This could be her song, although her mother would not be thrilled with her singing along.

'Oui. This play is good. Be joyful.' Jean snapped away while Charlotte swayed to the music. He clapped his hands. 'Good work. Next.'

Charlotte rushed to the change room for her next outfit while Jean changed the props on the stage. 'On y va. Let's get going,' Charlotte emerged with a white cotton blouse with flounced sleeves, black vest and silver belt over black trousers. A look that would get her a part in any Johnny Depp pirate movie, she mused.

'Formidable,' Jean proclaimed

After two more rounds of changes, Jean announced that they would be taking a short break before they started *Look Number Two*. This gave Charlotte time to grab a drink. Her jet lag had disappeared and she was on a high.

11

WHEN CHARLOTTE MET CHARLOTTE

Charlotte skipped out of the photographic studio and stumbled into a woman who was looking distractedly at her phone. The phone dropped and they both bent to pick it up, bumping heads in the process.

'Ouch!'

'Are you OK? Allez-vous bien? Charlotte inquired.

She looked into the woman's eyes and they both froze, transfixed by the near mirror image in front of them. They shared the same eyebrows and eye colour, nose, skin tone and facial structure. Charlotte's long tresses dipped in purple were a clear point of difference.

The woman standing opposite smiled, put out her hand and said simply,

'Charlotte.'

'Enchantée,' Charlotte replied with a huge grin on her face. 'Charlotte aussi.'

Bending over in a fit of giggles, a warm connection was made.

'Votre accent est un peu étrange. Your accent is a little strange.'

'Je suis Australienne,' Charlotte replied. 'Although I had an American grandmother I never knew.' She had no idea why she nervously mumbled this piece of information.

'Mon Dieu. Me too!' said the other woman.

'Êtes-vous un mannequin?'

'No, no. I'm not a model, well except for today. Je suis étudiante. I'm studying digital media. Je suis ici pour une histoire avec *Paris-Match*.'

'Moi aussi. I'm here for a story and photo shoot.'

They seemed to have a lot in common, although the other Charlotte's dress style was more Chanel and Dior than Charlotte's own downtown, Byron Bay, vintage-gypsy mix.

'Princesse?' A woman interrupted their conversation.

'I get called Princess a lot too,' Charlotte offered, 'but only by my dad, and only when he's not calling me Purple Head.'

The other Charlotte laughed and shook her head at the woman.

'Come. Let's take a coffee. I think we're going to be friends. Do you have time?'

'Yes. I've fifteen minutes before my photo shoot continues.'

'And after the photo shoot, what are your plans?'

'Not sure. I've still got to be interviewed for the article and tomorrow we take a tour of Paris for another photo shoot. We fly to Nice on Friday for another media engagement in Antibes. I'm going to meet a guy named Jacques. He's the reason I'm here, really. He's a deckhand on a yacht and he found a message in a bottle with a letter written to my brother, who died in an accident before I was born.'

'Mon Dieu! Goodness. It seems we share tragedy as well as looks. Maybe we are related?'

'Excusez-moi.' They were interrupted again by the well dressed and rather serious looking woman who put her finger on her watch and shrugged her shoulders.

'I have to go. But I live not far from Antibes. Call me after your photo shoot with the sailor and the bottle and I will collect you. We can then have a proper catch up.'

'Sounds lovely. I look forward to it.'

Chanel Charlotte passed her a business card, kissed her on both cheeks and waved goodbye. The words *Charlotte Casiraghi* were written in an elegant font with a phone number. She slipped the card into her pocket and went outside into the chilly spring air to grab a café au lait.

12

NOUVELLE CHARLIE

A New York-style skyline had arrived in the studio while Charlotte went for her coffee. It was amazing; hundreds of tiny lights hanging from the ceiling created a starry night spectacular, and there was a New York brownstone image on a curtain as a backdrop. Real stairs located in the middle of the set completed the transformation.

'Les cheveux. The hair,' Jean directed to Charlotte while pointing at an empty barber's chair in the corner. He followed her over, and the immaculately groomed goddess behind the chair started fondling her purple tipped tresses. 'So, we are ready for a change,' she whispered while holding up a section of hair, indicating a three-inch cut.

'Oui,' Charlotte tapped both shoulders with the tips of her fingers, signalling permission to remove five years of growth. 'Mais ici pour le changement.'

'Bravo Charlotte. On y va, Clarice,' Jean announced, lifting his arms as though he was commanding the ocean to part. And with that, Clarice commenced the conversion of country girl Charlotte into Chic Charlie.

Charlotte's hair was cut to shoulder length and wrapped up in chignon with threaded pearls and a black onyx comb. Mireille touched up her makeup, stuck on false eyelashes and applied a deep red lipstick. Jean held up two beautiful dresses for her to try on. The first was a classic, straight-line, above-the-knee black dress suitable for cocktail parties and fashion shows. The second was an emerald-green satin ball gown, with hidden seams of deep purple. There was a matching matador-style jacket. Charlotte slipped off the barber stool and sashayed over to Jean to take the dresses from his outstretched hand, while Clarice reached over to the music box and flooded the room with the distinctive sounds of the Pink Panther theme song. Everyone laughed.

'Parfait Charlotte. Parfait,' Jean cooed, clapping slowly. Clarice helped Charlotte slip on the black dress, adding a string of pearls, matching bracelet and oversized dark sunglasses. The reflection in the mirror was remarkable. Very Audrey Hepburn.

'Where's Charlotte Wyatt gone?' Charlotte whispered to herself. The music changed and she recognised the theme song from *Breakfast at Tiffany's* as it was one of Helen's favourites. Clarice pulled back the curtain to reveal *look number two* as Mason walked into the studio. He blinked, shook his head and stared at her transfixed. He then theatrically put his hand to his forehead and pretended to fall over as if in shock.

'Wow Miss Wyatt. Wow.' And then he started singing the old Sammy Davis Junior song *If My Friends Could See Me Now*.

'Your phone, Charlotte,' he demanded. 'Your parents won't believe me, or you, if you don't show them a snap of this – this remarkable transformation.' Charlotte beamed, and threw her phone across the room. Dropping into character, she daintily walked onto the set and reached up to touch one of the tiny lights. It looked as if she was reaching for the stars.

Mason took a number of photos using her phone, and then pulled up a chair to watch Jean direct her through a number of poses. She looked over her shoulder and winked at Mason, then glanced up at the lights, imagining a winter's evening in Byron Bay, before looking directly into the camera lens, oozing sensuality. She was having such fun pretending to be a confident woman of style and beauty. Hana joined them as Charlotte finished the last pose. She smiled and nodded at Mason and then at Charlotte. Jean chapped his hands and announced the last dress change of the session. Charlotte changed quickly with Clarice's help, and again respectfully followed Jean's instructions as he moved her through various poses.

'Bravo,' Hana called out when Jean announced that they were finished. After Charlotte changed clothes, she joined the others around a small table where they nibbled on a selection of cheeses, Provençal tarts and an onion and olive slice called pissaladière. Charlotte pinched herself, certain that she would wake up from this Cinderella fantasy at any moment.

'What's next?' she asked tentatively.

'You must see Paris. You cannot come across the ocean and only see inside *Paris-Match*.'

Hana looked at Mason.

'Drop your bags at your hotel and then take Charlotte to the Left Bank for a few snaps along the Seine, and then choose your favourite places. Jean will go with you to capture the memories. Make sure you visit wardrobe before you go.'

'Bien sûr,' Mason replied. 'Of course.'

'Then we can catch up over dinner. Au Bon Accueil at seven. My treat. We can review the story so far, discuss further photos needed and explore how to manage the meeting and the messages with Jacques when Charlotte finally collects la bouteille, the bottle.'

'Understood. A ce soir. Until tonight.'

Loaded with a few changes of clothes, Charlotte, Mason and Jean undertook a whirlwind tour of Paris, starting at the Eiffel Tower. The area was heavily congested with ice cream sellers, tourists, buskers and colourfully dressed Africans selling chintzy models of the Tower.

'You've gotta be kidding?' Charlotte said as Mason returned with two cones topped with vanilla and chocolate. Jean laughed.

'Makes a fun photo. Lean in and I'll take a couple of snaps,' Jean offered

'Alright, but only if you take some on my phone too.'

'Bien sûr.'

Charlotte passed her phone to Jean and returned to stand beside Mason, the famous French structure towering in the background. She was shivering, so Mason put his arm around her and they both leaned in together, licking their ice creams as Jean snapped away.

'OK. Enough. Finish eating your ice creams and let's go take a few photos on the Champs Elysées and the Seine.'

Charlotte loved the tree-lined street and sense of majesty as the Champs Elysées ran up to the Arc de Triomphe. Jean was able to capture Charlotte's sense of wonder at her surroundings in his shots. She did as she was told, moving her body, hands and facial expressions as directed. A crowd of onlookers started following them, taking photos of Jean taking photos of her. This amused Charlotte.

'I see you have your first paparazzi,' Mason remarked.

'I feel like I'm deceiving them. As if I'm a proper model.'

'C'est suffisant. That's enough for here,' Jean announced, folding his tripod.

The evening was drawing in so the trio took a boat cruising the Seine for a final photo shoot. Charlotte admired the street lights and how the city was sparkling as darkness descended. She squeezed into a toilet cubicle, to the bemusement of other women washing their hands and changed into a long, sequinned dress, with a puffy jacket streaming small pieces of white, silver and grey fabric, before adding diamante earrings and bracelet.

'Wow,' Mason whispered, snapping images on his smart phone. Jean again suggested poses for Charlotte as they passed by historical landmarks such as Notre Dame and the Musée d' Orsay. Again, a few people gathered to watch. As the numbers grew, so did Jean's annoyance as they began to get in his way.

'OK, we're done,' Jean suddenly announced. 'Well done Charlotte. I think I have gold in my camera. Call by tomorrow and I'll show you. For now, I get off at the next stop and go home.' Charlotte kissed him on both cheeks and Mason shook his hand.

'A demain. Tomorrow,' Jean said as he disembarked with his photographic equipment. The crowd melted away and Charlotte changed back into her jeans. She and Mason disembarked at the next stop and grabbed a taxi back to their hotel to drop off the clothing from the shoot and to change into more suitable clothes for dinner.

When they arrived at Bon Accueil forty minutes later they found Hana already there, seated at a table and talking on her phone. She waved them over as she concluded the call.

'Jean tells me that he captured many magical memories today, despite being challenged by your little paparazzi.'

Charlotte giggled. 'Yes, it did become a bit difficult for him. Must admit I felt awkward with everyone looking at me, so I just pretended they weren't there.'

'A good strategy which I'm certain you will need again. Particularly after our next edition comes out.'

'What advice do you have for managing *Les Papps*?' Charlotte asked, feeling a little nervous.

'Embrace them. Give them a wonderful pose and your best smile. They will make money from selling the picture, the word and images will spread and then we will make money as magazine sales increase. A beautiful image is what helps a story go viral.' Charlotte nodded at Hana and then at Mason, acknowledging his previous advice about the role of beauty in making a story go viral.

'A drink?' Hana asked, waving her heavily ring-laden hand in the direction of a nearby waiter without waiting for a response.

'Bien sûr,' Charlotte replied politely. 'Un verre de vin rouge peut-être?'

'I want red wine too,' Mason chipped in.

'Le Medoc,' Hana instructed the waiter.

While the waiter left to get the wine, Hana took another call and Mason excused himself to visit the bathroom. Charlotte skipped though the photos on her phone and smiled. She sent the photo of her wearing the evening dress and pearls on the New York-styled set to her parents.

Do you recognise the girl in the picture?

Moments later the phone pinged. Her parents were awake early.

Nope. Wow. Who is she? She's exquisite. A famous Parisian model perhaps?

Not yet. (^-^*)

Charlotte's thoughts turned to Miranda. She regretted taking so few photos on the trip so far. There was only one of Mason. She selected it and started typing.

Been super busy. Suspect you have too as I've not heard from you?
Snap of me and Mason under the Eiffel Tower. Way too cold for ice cream.
Looking forward to hearing from you.

A few minutes later she received an uncharacteristically short reply.

I see that Mason is keeping you warm?

Charlotte looked up and saw Mason in the far corner of the restaurant, talking on his phone. Miranda had got the wrong message. Mason was a family friend – no more than that. Or was he? She put her phone down feeling confused.

The waiter was pouring three glasses of wine after Hana tasted a little and confirmed it was *acceptable*. Mason pulled out his chair and sat down.

'Just briefing Jane on the day's activities. She's keen to see the photos and how we link the London, Paris and Antibes stories together.'

'Yes. Important. Your thoughts on messages to accompany the photos?'

Mason described his ideas for half a dozen articles which would be drip fed on social media to build global interest in the story. Hana listened with interest. 'Good. I like these. And can I suggest that when you meet with the sailor ...' Hana outlined her thoughts on how to create the right mood for when Charlotte received the bottle. She was also keen for Mason to not let the journalist from *Nice-Matin* take all the photos. Mason scribbled the instructions into a small, black Moleskine notebook then looked back at Hana and nodded. Hana signalled to the waiter to refill their glasses.

'Tell me, Mason,' Hana asked, swirling the wine around in her glass, 'How did you two meet?'

He moved his hands to his mouth, looked at Charlotte and grimaced.

'I don't know to be honest. We both have family in Byron Bay. It's not a big town. Everyone knows everyone. Perhaps it was at a surf carnival that we first met? The girls were in the Byron Bay Surf Club too. In fact, I seem to recall that you're quite a good swimmer aren't you Charlotte. Though, perhaps not good enough to out-swim a shark.'

'Mon dieu!' Hana shrieked.

'It's not what it seems, Hana,' Charlotte replied in exasperation, punching him in the arm. 'This is a bone I still need to pick with your mate Scott next time I see him. In fact, the last time I saw you both was six years ago when everyone got a little skittish about a couple of sharks cruising around Julian Rocks. Trust me. It's not that interesting a story.'

'Really? I do not understand you Australians,' Hana offered, shaking her head before emptying her glass in one gulp. 'Tell me Charlotte, what are your future plans? Will you be a champion swimmer, shark expert or model?'

'None of those,' she said, laughing 'although I would like to work in fashion.'

'Then, when you are ready, you must call me. I can make introductions.'

'Je le ferai. Absolutely, I will do that.' Charlotte beamed.

Mason looked at his watch.

'We should head off as we have another full day tomorrow.' As if on cue, Charlotte yawned. 'We'll drop off the clothes from the shoot tomorrow morning, and call by to get any last-minute instructions before we head to the airport.'

'All sounds good. Sleep well, you two,' Hana offered with a twinkle in her eye. Charlotte and Mason knew what Hana was intimating. They kissed her on both cheeks and started the walk back to the hotel in silence. When they were two blocks from the hotel, they heard shouts from a few inebriated men arguing over a referee's decision in a football game. The revellers' attention was distracted when one of them noticed Charlotte and called out to her. Instinctively Mason wrapped his arm around her and pulled her close.

The men whistled as they walked past. Mason did not release her until they were safely inside the hotel's reception.

'That was appreciated, Mason, but not necessary. You're not my protector.'

'Ah but I am,' he replied. 'I got the hard word from your mum.'

'What is it with you and my mum and Scott Harmon and my mum? It's like you're in some secret club that I'm not a member of.'

Mason laughed. 'No, not a club, but definitely there's a connection. We met your mum when we were small. We were swimming in the shallows at Byron Bay and Scott started talking to your mum as if she was a lost mermaid. I didn't hear all the conversation, but she did seem to be a mystical water creature to us. Then we met again later when Scott's gran married your grandpa.'

'That still doesn't explain the strong connection.'

'There's nothing more I can tell you. We just made this connection at the beach and when your mum realised I was your contact in London she asked me to look out for you. If you need to know more, you'll need to ask Scott next time you see him, or better still – ask your mum.'

They stepped into the tiny elevator and were very aware of how intimate the environment was as the lift rose judderingly slowly to the fifth floor. There was an awkward moment as they both turned the keys in their respective doors, and hesitated before entering, unsure of what to say.

'Breakfast at 8:00?' Charlotte offered. Mason smiled, feeling relieved that the awkward moment had passed.

'Oui,' he replied. 'A demain. See you in the morning'

Charlotte slumped on the bed looking at the photos and

messages on her phone. It was easy to see why Miranda misconstrued the photo under the Eiffel Tower. She reread the message from Miranda and started typing.

Nope. Not keeping me warm. More soon.

Hopefully, that would allay Miranda's fears.

13

OFF TO NICE

'Yes. These three images are the best. I adore them. Merci Jean.' Hana was smiling while Jean was looking smug. 'Now I look forward to the story. Well, stories in fact. You promised me four, Mason, and I need them tout de suite, very soon. So allez. Go. You two had best be off or you will miss your flight. Call me tonight to update me on the sailor and the story. I want to know everything.'

'Bien sûr,' they replied as they rushed to pick up their bags.

Mason put on his earphones and Charlotte looked out the window at the sprawling suburbs of Paris as the plane ascended. What a lovely city, she thought. I'm leaving it before I've had time to experience all it has to offer. Not wanting to lose a single memory, she turned on her device to note down her thoughts.

. . .

Reflective Journal – Leaving Paris – 22 March

In 24 hours, this city has made quite the impression.
So many old and beautiful buildings with playful
flourishes and towers reaching high.
Buildings like Notre Dame and the Musée d'Orsay
stand proudly on the river bank.
I'm in awe.
And then there are the bridges. Beautiful bridges.
We floated underneath.

A magical setting for me to pretend to be someone
else.
And it's not so easy pretending to be a model.

But Mason cheered me on. At times making me
laugh.
When we left London, we were just acquaintances.
People from the same town with shared connections.
Now. I don't know.

After our time together, I now feel that we're friends.
Good friends. Mates.

He's not my type. Goodness. What am I thinking?
He's Miranda's man – well he will be, once he gets to
spend time with her and see how lovely and funny
she is.
If only they didn't live on opposite sides of the world.

Charlotte's eyes flickered guiltily towards Mason. He still had on his headphones and was typing on his computer. She leaned in closer.

This story will capture the imagination of anyone who dreams of discovering far off places and making connections ...

Mason looked up and Charlotte leaned back in her seat without reading any more. She felt awkward for having read what he was writing without asking permission.

'Soon,' he said. 'Soon you and the entire world will read this story. For the moment, it's still being created.' The plane dipped to the right and Charlotte gasped as they flew over the sparkling sea and arrived into Nice airport with a gentle thump on the tarmac.

A thin, wispy-looking young man stood at the back of the crowd at arrivals holding up a sign saying NICE-MATIN for WYATT– MURRAY.

'Julien,' Mason offered, thrusting out his hand through the crowds. 'And this is Charlotte. We're here to meet a boat, collect a bottle and take a few photos.'

'Welcome to the Côte d'Azur,' Julien offered, shaking their hands. 'How long are you here for?'

'Just the day. We fly back to London tomorrow.'

'So short. Quel dommage. What a pity. You will not be able to see very much of the French Riviera.'

'I know. And we've not seen very much of Paris either. We're disappointed. But you know, this is a work trip,' Mason said in his most sensible sounding voice. Julien smiled and shrugged his shoulders before picking up Charlotte's bag. He grimaced.

'Mon Dieu! This is not a bag for a short visit.' They all laughed.

Julien dropped them at the hotel with instructions to get changed and refresh Charlotte's makeup and rendezvous at the Ferris wheel beside the port of Antibes in fifteen minutes. Charlotte dressed as instructed by Hana, in a white sailor's shirt with matching jacket and trousers. She felt the look was contrived and did not feel comfortable. It didn't matter. This was the last time that she would be dressing up and pretending to be someone else.

It had just passed two o'clock as they left their rendezvous point to walk along the old walls of Antibes and down to the far end of the port. There were hundreds of leisure craft gently bobbing in the water.

'Wow. These are beautiful,' Charlotte observed. 'I could easily live on any of these.'

'Wait until you see the super yachts,' Julien offered, pointing to a pier fifty metres ahead that was partly obscured behind an old wall. They arrived at a locked security gate. Julien shook it and called out to a person standing near the edge of the pier, about twenty metres away. The attendant turned around, extinguished his cigarette and nonchalantly strolled over to open the gate.

Charlotte was in awe of the monolithic vessels lined up along the pier. The yachts were magnificent, shiny constructions, with multiple levels, many with motorboats and jet skis secured on a lower deck. Several even had helicopters parked on an upper level.

'There it is,' Julien called out.

His cry caught the attention of a sailor standing alone near the top of the gangplank. He looked towards the trio without acknowledging them and walked down the gangplank and towards Charlotte, ignoring her companions. He was a little taller than Charlotte, deeply tanned, and with his wavy, shoulder-length, dirty-blonde hair pulled back in a ponytail. He walked towards her, his eyes locked on hers, reached out for her hand and kissed it gently.

'Belle. You are beautiful,' he said softly. 'No one told me you were beautiful.' Charlotte was lost for words. Mason cringed.

'Jacques, I assume?' Julien asked.

'Oui. Mais, Jack to my friends – and I hope we will be friends.' Once again he addressed Charlotte, ignoring both Julien and Mason.

'Where are we going to have this photo shoot?' Mason asked.

'Viens. Come with me. The bottle is on the boat.'

They followed Jacques up the gangplank and into a large sunken room with timber flooring and a dozen black leather chairs with white, purple and grey cushions. There was no longer a sense of being on a yacht. Instead they felt they were in a room designed to welcome heads of state and royalty. There was a long black granite table set up with a silver tray of colourful drinks and exotic fruit. Julien moved to set up his camera tripod.

'Not yet,' Jacques cautioned. 'Let her read the letter first.' Julien nodded, stepped away from his tripod and pulled out his notebook to review the questions he planned to ask Charlotte. Jacques signalled for Julien and Mason to sit down. They followed his instructions while watching him carefully. Mason was a little surprised by Jacques' confidence. It was not what he had expected from a deckhand. Jacques signalled for Charlotte to sit beside him on the opposite sofa and passed her the bottle. She held it gingerly, pondering the long journey it had made from the other side of the world. Inside she could see a cream parchment. She removed the cork and turned the bottle upside down to coax it out. It obeyed. The click of a camera momentarily dragged her eyes away from the bottle to Julien.

'Non. Not yet,' Jacques directed at Julien with annoyance.

'I must,' he replied, 'this moment is important to capture.'

Jacques looked at Charlotte.

'It's OK. Let them take their photos. It's what was agreed. But thank you for your concern.' Jacques shrugged his shoulders and stood to leave.

'No, no, no. Please stay where you are, Jacques,' Julien asserted.

'Non,' Jacques replied firmly. 'This story is not about me.'

'Au contraire, you are a key part of this bottle's journey.' An awkward silence hung in the air for a moment while the trio waited a reply from Jacques.

'D'accord. OK,' he said finally. 'The best photo can be taken from over my shoulder towards Charlotte.'

'I do not agree,' Julien retorted.

'I do not care. You do not have a contract with me.'

Julien was startled but recognised the truth of what Jacques was saying. He was beginning to feel nervous that he would not capture the images he needed for the story.

'Of course, we will focus on Charlotte,' Mason intervened between the two hot-headed, Gallic men. Julien moved behind Jacques to take photos over his shoulder.

Charlotte was reading the first of the two documents that had fallen from the bottle.

If I had to bury my son,
I would hope that I was one hundred and ten
And that he had enjoyed the rich life he deserved.
And that standing here today
I would have wonderful stories to share
Of sandcastles built and races run along the beach.

But this was not to be your story.
My heart is breaking
That all I have to share with you
Is knowledge of how much you were loved.

I want you to know
That I was waiting for you
Your room was *nearly* ready
And that I had already briefed you
while you were in my womb
On all the things we were going to do together.

It was going to be a wonderful life.

But now I need to find a new path
Without you on this journey
I'll never forget you
And will think of you every day
And I hope that each time you hear
The roar of thunder and rain falling to the earth
That you will remember
That these are my tears

Flowing into a never-ending river of love for you.

Charlotte caught her breath as she was momentarily transported to a time before she was born; to a time of great loss in her parents' life of which she knew very little. There was another note, handwritten this time on a smaller piece of paper.

To darling Scott,

You only lived a day but we will remember you forever.
While you are gone from our lives – you will never be gone from our hearts.

Mum and Dad
Byron Bay, Australia

Charlotte's throat constricted and she knew that tears were not far from the surface. She looked at Mason who was looking at her with concern. A machine gun round of clicks exploded from Julien's camera. Jacques growled and Charlotte gave him a dismissive nod to demonstrate that she was fine. She held the bottle close for a further round of photos and allowed him to snap images of the notes from the bottle. She was aware that while the letter was written by her parents, the eulogy was written by her mother. A cough from the far doorway distracted her.

'Jack, we weigh anchor in an hour.' Jacques nodded at his colleague and reached out for Charlotte's hand. He cradled it gently.

'Have you seen much of Antibes?'

'Not yet,' Charlotte replied with a smile.

'Viens. Come with me. Time is short. Let me give you

some lovely memories before you go.' Without referring to either Mason or Julien, he passed her a bag to put the bottle and letters in. She stood up and he took her hand in his, led her out of the stateroom and down the gangplank. Julien quickly disassembled his tripod and followed. He and Mason had to walk quickly to keep up with the pair who were now under the archway in the ramparts surrounding the old town of Antibes. Julien was particularly anxious as he hadn't yet asked any questions for the article and he needed to get back to the office. He rushed up to the pair and attempted to walk in synchronisation with them.

'Charlotte please, a few questions for you ...'

'Of course.'

'When did your parents tell you about the bottle?'

'They didn't. We'll be having quite the conversation when I get home.'

'How did you find out about the bottle?'

'I became suspicious when I found Mason's post about a bottle from Byron Bay being scooped out of the sea near France while I was researching an assignment on what makes a story go viral. We literally, had reporters knocking on our door five minutes later.'

'How did the reporters find you – I mean your parents?

'I don't know and that's a good question. I guess someone did a thorough piece of investigative journalism, perhaps looking through the registry of deaths in Byron Bay. And of course there are people in the area who knew about my brother's death. Mason, do you have any ideas?'

Mason shook his head.

'Interesting,' Julien mused while scribbling furiously.

'Wow,' Charlotte cooed as they reached the top of the rampart walls and looked out across a small beach to the Cap d'Antibes stretching around in a curve on the right. The sea was a beautiful dark blue with sporadic white frosty waves.

'It's easy to see why this is the called the Côte d'Azur, n'est-ce pas.'

'Absolumente,' Charlotte replied. 'Oh, I wish we could stay longer.'

'So do I,' Mason chimed in. 'Let's grab a beer later and talk about whether we could stay a bit longer.'

'Agreed.'

Jacques looked at his watch.

'I need to get back to the yacht. Will you accompany me?'

'Bien sûr. Of course,' Charlotte replied as she accepted the offer of Jacque's elbow.

Mason and Julien raised their eyebrows at each other in dismay. It was as if they weren't there.

'One final question for you, Jacques. Where did you find the bottle?' Julien asked

'Well, in the sea of course.' He smiled cheekily, knowing that he was frustrating the journalist.

'But what were you doing?'

'I was swimming. The boat was anchored and I had a thirty-minute break. I went for a dip and just as I was about to climb back inside, the sunlight bounced off the bottle and caught my eye.'

'So, you went to retrieve it, intrigued by what might be inside?' Julien offered.

'No. I swam out to get the bottle as the ocean has enough rubbish.'

Julien did not record Jacques response.

'That's all good then. Thank you. How do you want me to refer to you in the article?'

Jacques viewed Julien thoughtfully. 'Jack. You can call

me Jack. Jack Dee.'

'That's not a very French name?' Julien queried.

'It is what it is. Jacques was the name of my grandfather. It's an old family name. Jack is fine.' Julien's nose crinkled with irritation at his response.

'You know Jack Dee is the name of a British comedian?' Mason offered.

'Well, There are only so many names in the world,' he shrugged, dismissively.

'I must leave now, Mason, I'll let you know when I have the article and photos ready. Can you do the same?

'Of course. And thanks for the collection service from the airport. It was appreciated.'

'My pleasure. However, I can't take you back to the airport tomorrow as I'm in the Var. Make sure you don't take a taxi. They're robber barons. A train is better. Take the train from Antibes to Nice St Augustin and then walk a little way to the airport. It's not far although I know you have *rather heavy* luggage,' he added with a smile. Charlotte was out of earshot as she was deeply engrossed in whatever Jacques was whispering in her ear.

'We'll manage together,' Mason replied, 'and thanks again.' The men shook hands and Julien walked back out under the arch and turned left in the direction of the underground car park. Mason turned right and had to sprint to catch up to Jacques and Charlotte, who were now approaching the entrance to the super yacht pier. By the time he reached them they were saying their goodbyes.

'Can we have a last photo before you go? Mason enquired. Jacques nodded and put his arm around Charlotte's waist and pulled her close. She looked in his eyes and he leant forward and unexpectedly kissed her. It was soft and lingering and literally took her breath away. Mason took one photo and stopped. He felt embarrassed, intruding on a private moment, but recognised that the photo was public relations gold. The embrace ended and Jacques kept his gaze firmly on Charlotte.

'Look after that bottle. There's a message for you inside the bag.' Charlotte nodded, unable to respond as she was still remembering the feel of his lips on hers. Mason shuffled forward and shook Jacques' hand.

'Thanks Jack, for being available for the interview.'

'My pleasure.'

'How will we contact you, to let you know about the story?'

'Charlotte will know.' Charlotte looked at Mason and shrugged her shoulders, not understanding what he was saying, and turned to Jacques, who had run up the gangplank.

'Have a good journey home Charlotte. Au revoir.'

Her head was spinning. Jacques disappeared inside and moments later the gangplank was retracted and the yacht made a slow and gracious departure from its berth. As it turned and headed out to sea it passed another yacht that was now moving into the vacated place on the pier. Charlotte stared at Jacques' yacht until it was out of view.

'Ready to go?' Mason asked. Charlotte nodded and Mason put a comforting arm around her shoulders. They turned and started walking back to their hotel when a cry caught their attention.

'Is that the Mighty Murray?'

Mason grinned and looked back towards the new yacht. Charlotte was momentarily confused. Someone was waving from the lower level.

'Beam me up, Scotty,' Mason called out.

'No need. I'm taking the shuttle.' Mason laughed and did

a funny skip on the spot before walking over to meet his friend.

'Fancy meeting you here.' They hugged and did some vigorous back slapping as was a common ritual among Australian males. Charlotte guessed that the person in the smart uniform was Scott Harmon but didn't immediately recognise him with trimmed hair and a crisp white uniform. Last time she'd seen him was six years ago when he was wearing a black wetsuit and life jacket and riding a jet ski. She'd been happily swimming on her own, one hundred metres off Main Beach when he'd insisted that she climb aboard for a ride. Charlotte hated jet skis and was fairly sure that Scott just wanted to 'save her' as he'd done when she was ten years old and caught in a rip. She finally acquiesced and was irritated to discover, when they reached the shore, that everyone was being asked to evacuate the water because a few grey nurse sharks were circling Julian Rocks.

'Why didn't you tell me?' she'd demanded.

'I didn't want to send you into a panic where you'd start thrashing about.'

'You should have given me more credit than that,' she had responded angrily. 'I'm also a lifesaver.'

'I keep forgetting,' he'd replied, 'to me you're just little ...'

'Charlie Girl,' she completed his sentence with annoyance before stomping up the beach. That was the last time she'd seen him. Until today. She looked at Mason laughing loudly at something Scott had said. He waved her over.

'Hey, come and join us.'

'Who's this?' Scott asked.

'Guess?'

Scott looked momentarily confused. 'You're not Charlie Girl?'

'No. I'm not Charlie Girl. I'm Charlotte. Charlotte Wyatt.'

'Forgive me. I didn't recognise you. You've grown so ... so tall since I last saw you.'

'Funny that.'

'I can see that. I can see that you're now a sailor.'

Charlotte looked at what she was wearing and suppressed a smile. 'No not a sailor. Just a courier, collecting a message in a bottle for my brother.'

'Sir,' came a shout from the yacht. 'You're needed.'

'I've gotta go. This is an unscheduled stop for repairs, and I need to brief the crew. Can we meet at the Hop Store in an hour?'

'You bet. As long as you tell us where it is.'

Scott smiled, gave them directions and went back aboard the yacht, leaving Charlotte and Mason free to return to their hotel. The day was drawing to an end and the temperature was dropping. Charlotte was pleased to change into clothes that were warmer and more sens d'elle-même, her own style.

14
____

THE HOP STORE

'There you go.' Scott placed three pints of Guinness on the large wooden table in the pub. Charlotte and Mason barely noticed as they finished counting their money.

'That makes twelve euros, nine pounds and ten Aussie dollars. Think you'll need to buy the next round too, mate,' Mason said to Scott, grimacing as he pushed his glasses back up his nose.

'No worries. What are you guys saving up for?'

'Eating, a roof over our head. You know, luxuries like that.'

'Aren't you going back to London tomorrow?

'We are, but we'd like to stay longer. Seems a pity to go back when I can work from here and Charlotte doesn't fly back to Brissie until Sunday. However, we're a bit low on funds and we've maxed out our credit cards.'

'I see. Well, I think it's your lucky day. I believe I can see my way clear to advance you a few shekels for beer money, and more importantly, we now have a few beds available on board with my crew having an unexpected shore leave break. As long as you're OK with rather narrow bunks – you can crash there.'

'That would be brilliant.'

'And so consistent with your lifesaver role,' Charlotte offered with more than a dollop of sarcasm. Scott wondered what he'd done to annoy her. She'd changed so much in six years and he couldn't quite get used to the beautiful young woman she had morphed into. She was no longer his sister's freckle-faced friend. He suddenly remembered Miranda's last WhatsApp message.

'So Miranda said something about a message in a bottle. That's why you're here?

'Yep. That's right. Bottle collected,' she replied, with a curious grin as she lifted up the bag Jacques had given her to carry the bottle. 'Mason's writing it up.' She reached inside the bag and pulled out the bottle. A small white business card fluttered to the ground. Mason reached down to pick it up.

Jacques Dessault
+ 33 (0) 662 007 007

'I see that our Jack Dee is a double, double oh seven whose real name is Jacques Dessault. Maybe he's not a deckhand at all but a French spy? How exciting.'

'Gimme that, Mason,' Charlotte demanded. She looked at the card and then at the reverse side. There were no other contact details. Puzzled, she slipped the card back into the bag. 'I think you're jealous,' she added.

'What is it with you two?' Scott asked. 'Are you having a lovers' tiff?'

Charlotte looked at Mason and then at Scott.

'Well, we have slept together.' Mason roared with laughter and reached over and kissed her on the cheek.

'Not in here, mate,' came a booming voice with a heavy Irish accent from behind the bar. They turned their attention to the tall barman with black rimmed glasses who was pointing at a sign behind the bar that said, *No kissing in the bar unless with staff.* Charlotte was now laughing so hard she nearly dropped the bottle. Scott reached across to steady it.

'May I?' he asked. She nodded and released the bottle. He examined it closely while Charlotte examined Scott. His blonde hair was short at the back with a widow's peak on his forehead and a sweep of hair flicked to the right like a fabulous wave. From his lean body she guessed that he was still managing to surf. She recognised his blue eyes with their distinctive smattering of grey speckles and he stroked his chin in that familiar way when he was concentrating, as he was now.

'What's written inside?'

'There's a eulogy for my brother from my mother and a letter reminding him that he will always be loved. You can read it if you like.'

Scott shook his head. 'Sounds personal. Doesn't feel right.'

'Of all the people in our lives I'd think mum would least object to you reading the letter. And besides, soon everyone will know what it says.' Scott said nothing and passed the bottle back.

'Did you see my brother before he died?' He shook his head.

'The first time I met your mother he wasn't born. And

the second time I met her she was at George's house recovering from the accident. I was only four at the time, but I remember how fragile she was, like a bird that had fallen from a tree and broken its wings. She could hardly walk, let alone fly.' He paused. 'She seemed very pleased to see me, even though we'd only met once – when I thought she was a mermaid. Do you remember that day on the beach, Mason?' He nodded.

'So, was my brother named after you?'

'Seems unlikely.'

'Maybe you made more of an impression than you thought.'

He shrugged his shoulders. 'You'll need to ask her. Changing the topic completely, what are you going to do now you've extended your stay on The Riviera?'

Charlotte smiled and bit her bottom lip, looking at Mason with anticipation.

'Before we make plans, I need to make a call. I've a friend here who told me I should contact her. After that, I'm open to suggestions.'

'Righty-ho. Go call her.'

Charlotte went outside to make the call and when she returned, Scott was sitting on his own.

'We're having coffee on Saturday morning,' she reported

'Good oh.'

'Where's Mason?'

'He's gone to call his boss to let her know about the change of plan.'

'What about your plans, Scott? Will you be able to join us?'

'I hope so. I have calls to make to suppliers, repairs to oversee and route planning to complete. I'll need a couple of hours.'

'It's a pretty responsible job, being captain of such an impressive boat.'

'It's not a boat, it's a ship. A yacht. And I'm not captain. Not yet anyway. I'm hoping to get my license later this year.'

'You don't want to be a marine biologist then?'

That's what he'd studied at uni, she remembered.

'Yeah, well, I'm still into creatures from the deep. But I wanted a break after uni.'

'Yeah, Helen said you ran out of money on your round-the-world trip.'

'Doesn't everyone?' he laughed. 'Yeah, so that's when I got a job as a deckhand. The money's not bad and I worked my way up. I love sailing.'

'What'll you do next?'

'Ah, I dunno. After I get my captain's license we'll see. The maritime world is full of opportunities. Indeed, the world is full of possibilities.' He paused, looking at her. 'And you. What are you doing now?

'Still studying. Started with fashion design and got a bit disillusioned because of the lack of jobs. Switched to Digital Media Studies as the job market was more promising. But on this trip, I've been reminded how much I love fashion. And I've loved the travel. I've been to London and Paris and here and now I'm itching to get out and see more. Mum and Dad would have a fit if I told them. Was hard getting their go ahead for this trip. Mum particularly is so afraid of losing me, you know, after losing my brother.'

Mason pulled out his chair and sat down with a gloomy expression on his face.

'We can't stay?' Charlotte asked.

'Yeah we can stay, but I have to get all the articles finished and sent to Jane by lunch time tomorrow.'

'That sounds reasonable, mate. Why the long face?'

'I'm pissed off. I thought that trusting us to work remotely applied to everyone. Seems she's suspicious of my ability to work down here with all the temptations of the Côte d'Azur.'

'How long have you worked for her?'

'Three months.'

'Then her caution is understandable. Prove her wrong! Settle down and get the stuff written. Over-deliver on what you promised. Then you'll have her respect and we'll have time to play.'

'You're right.' Mason patted his friend on the shoulder and reached for his jacket.

'If you're bunkering down for a couple of hours, I'll spend time on my assignment too.' Charlotte remarked.

'Come on then. Let me pick up some pizza sustenance for all the worker bees,' Scott offered. Charlotte smiled, looking at Scott as he put his coat on. He was quite different to the person she remembered from Byron Bay.

Messages home later that evening

> **Message to Mum and Dad.** *Got the bottle today and am currently in hotel working on uni assignment Bumped into Scott Harmon at Antibes port. He says Hi.*

> **Response from Mum.** *How lovely. Please give Scott a hug from me. Love Mum*

> **Message to Miranda.** *Guess what?*

> **Response from Miranda.** *You've met up with my brother in France.*

Response Charlotte. *Yep. Total surprise. He's cool and generous and now Mason and I can spend the weekend on the Riviera.*

Response from Miranda. *I heard that too. And that you and Mason had slept together.*

Response Charlotte. *No. Well yes. You've got the wrong end of the stick. Can I call you to explain?*

Silence.

15

A DAY ON THE CÔTE D'AZUR

'Done!' Mason announced as he met Charlotte in the hotel's reception at eleven the following morning. 'Jane's pleased so I'm sorted. And I remembered to call Hana and update her too. How'd you go?'

'Assignment not finished, but solid progress made.'

'Great. Sounds like we can begin our Riviera adventure, after we've dropped off our luggage on the yacht.' He was grinning like he'd won the lottery.

Scott was waiting for them on the pier. His eyes flickered towards her large bag and then at her. He smiled. She knew what he was thinking. Charlotte had become quite adept at dragging her big bag behind her and at ignoring the looks and jibes of her male companions.

'Really?' he offered.

'I did tell you I had a thing for clothes.'

'You are true to your word.'

'And you are not discreet with yours.'

'What?'

'I have a bone to pick with you.'

'Mate, can you take the bags down below. It seems I need to have a private word with Miss Wyatt.' Mason picked up the bags and carefully headed down the stairs.

'What's up Charlie Girl?'

'Again. I'm not Charlie Girl. Indeed, I'm not anyone's girl. Yes, I slept with Mason, but not in the biblical sense. If it's any of your business I fell asleep on his bed, and he was such a gentleman that he didn't wake me to ask me to decamp to the sofa. Further, your sister is rather fond of your best friend and you've upset her by telling her we're involved.'

'Oh dear.'

'Is that all you can say?'

He started laughing, and then stopped. 'I'm sorry. I'm really sorry. You must admit this is funny. I ... I really don't know you very well, even though I've known you a long time. I didn't know if it was a joke when you said you'd slept with Mason. When Miranda asked me directly if you two were involved I said I didn't know, although you'd admitted that you'd slept together. I didn't think before I spoke. So again, please accept my apologies. I'll set my sister straight.'

'Thank you,' Charlotte replied. A squeak on the gang-plank signalled Mason's return.

'Small, cosy and acceptable, Mr Harmon.'

'I'm pleased it meets your standards, mate. Are you ready to see a bit more of the Côte D'Azur?'

'Too right I am. All good here?' he asked, looking directly at Charlotte. She smiled.

'All good here too. Let's go.'

. . .

Scott had borrowed a local crew member's car for the afternoon. He drove them through the old town of Antibes and along the ramparts, around the Cap d'Antibes surrounded by glorious homes and umbrella-like pine trees, past the famous Hotel du Cap-Eden-Roc, favoured haunt of movie stars, and into the beach resort of Juan les Pins.

'Can we stroll a bit, Scott?' Charlotte asked, leaning out the window taking photos.

'Absolutely. Let's do that at Cannes where we'll cruise the Croisette, stop for lunch and engage in some serious people watching.' Charlotte beamed. They parked under the Palais des Festivals and emerged beside the port of Cannes. Like the port of Antibes there was a large array of beautiful craft sitting calmly in the water. Her eyes ran along the row of restaurants on the water's edge and then up a hill to where a château was perched. There were old men playing boules and artists selling paintings and jewellery in the town square.

'Where to start. I want to go everywhere.'

'I'll do the best I can,' Scott said, smiling. 'This way first.'

The three Australians walked towards the Palais des Festivals, well known for the annual Cannes Film Festival. They took photos of the handprints and signatures of hundreds of movie stars who had left their mark in concrete on the sidewalk. On reaching the famous red carpeted staircase, Charlotte seized the opportunity to slink up the steps, pretending to be a nominee for the Palme D'Or, the most prestigious prize at the festival. She gave a regal wave to her compatriots when she reached the top and pretended to lift her long gown to avoid tripping.

'You do that very well,' Mason mused as she bounced down the steps two at a time to join them.

'Gotta get in some practice in case our bottle's journey becomes a blockbuster movie.'

'Well, that would be a measure of a truly viral story. Which reminds me, we must buy a copy of today's *Nice-Matin* to see how Julien described your encounter with Monsieur Jacques.' Scott directed them to a small marchand de journaux on the Croisette where they purchased several copies. The front cover featured the photo taken over Jack's shoulder with Charlotte looking pensively at the bottle for the first time. The heading was *Une bouteille d'amour,* A bottle of love. On the third page there were additional photos of Charlotte reading the letter and the poem, with a translation provided in French. The photos were good and the description short and factual. Mason was pleased.

'While we won't be first to market, we will have a more intriguing photo and story to share. I think you'd better wear your dark glasses and put your hat on to avoid being recognised.' Charlotte laughed and the trio continued along the Croisette, observing the people enjoying the spring sunshine. Scott led them past the famous Carlton and Majestic hotels, up rue d'Antibes a popular shopping street, until they reached rue Hoche, a pedestrianised street lined with cafés and restaurants. After a delicious lunch spent watching the locals dressed in their finery and walking their tiny poodles, the trio walked past the Marche Forville, around le Suquet and climbed the hill to take in the view.

'What are the islands called?' Charlotte asked, pointing out to sea.

'Îles de Lérins is the collective name for the islands; the smaller inhabited island is Sainte-Honorat and the larger one Sainte-Marguerite. Île Sainte-Marguerite is most famous because it's where The Man in the Iron Mask was reportedly held prisoner in the fortress.'

'How dreadful and interesting at the same time. I'd love to visit.'

'You're in danger of feeling homesick if you go. The islands are covered in eucalyptus trees, just like home.' Charlotte smiled and Scott looked at his watch. 'We don't have time today, but one day.'

'What's next on the itinerary?'

'A drive along the coast to La Napoule and then we head inland to visit the beautiful villages of Valbonne and Mougins.'

'Sounds great. On y va. Let's get going.'

Message to Mum and Dad later than day

Awesome day. Scott is a very good tour guide. He drove Mason and I to famous seaside towns and medieval villages. Have had time to work on assignment and Mason has written his articles. Catching up with a friend tomorrow. See you Tuesday.

Message to Miranda

Here are three musketeers on hill in Cannes. Having fab time but keep remembering wonderful kiss from charming French sailor. Think I'm in love? See attached photo by Mason.

Message from Miranda

Need more information about spunky sailor and kiss. p.s Received note from Scott setting me straight about Mason. Sorry I misinterpreted stuff.

Message to Miranda

No worries. More tomorrow.
(*´ ‿ ` *)

16

MEETING UP WITH A FRIEND

Charlotte listened to the early morning sounds of the port as she devoured her third croissant. With the misunderstanding with Miranda sorted, life felt better.

'What's the plan for the day, me beauties?' Mason offered in a not too convincing pirate voice.

'You've forgotten I'm catching up with my friend over coffee. Not sure how long I'll be, so don't include me in your plans.'

'Who's your friend?' Scott asked, topping up her tea mug.

'Her name's Charlotte too. I met her outside the ladies' loos at *Paris-Match* and we just clicked as we had so much in common.'

'And her last name?'

'Does it matter?' Charlotte huffed annoyed. She picked up her bag to look for the card with her friend's name.'

'You can't be too cautious. Who knows what her intentions are? You could be robbed.'

'Been there. Done that.'

'What!'

'At the Gare du Nord after we'd hopped off the train and were looking for the best way to get to the office. I was tired and frustrated at waiting in line to buy a ticket and two backpackers offered to help me. Or so I thought. But they robbed me instead.'

'Did you fight back?'

'In a manner of speaking, yes. I reported them to the police, they were caught, and I got my money back. No fighting needed.'

'And do you know how to defend yourself if you need to?'

Charlotte shook her head.

'After you've finished your fourth croissant, I'll show you a few moves.'

'And I think we should develop a code,' Mason chipped in.

'What do you mean?'

'A trust rating. For example, if you feel that someone might be dodgy you can say *my TR* is dropping.'

'I think you watch too much Star Trek,' Charlotte replied. Mason smiled.

'Not possible. Tell me, what would you have scored the two backpackers with this rating system?'

'Hard to say. They were like me in terms of age. They understood my frustrations over queuing. I had no reason to mistrust them. I think a neutral TR score of five out of ten.'

'That score won't help you make a decision. Let's try another example. This new friend you met outside the bathroom in Paris. How would you rate her on trust?'

'I liked her.'

'That shouldn't figure in the calculation.'

'She was smartly dressed ...'

'And how does that relate to trust? She still could have been a well-dressed shyster.'

'Where does she live?'

'I don't know.' Charlotte fumbled around in the zipped compartments of her bag. 'Great, found her card. Bother. No address.'

'That automatically drops the score then,' Mason piped in.

'Last name?

'It's long and starts with a C and I doubt I can pronounce it correctly. Looks Italian.'

'Give that to me,' Scott reached out to signal that this was not a request. Charlotte handed him the card. His eyebrow lifted as he looked at the name and telephone number and then flipped the card to see if anything was written on the back.

'I think you should Google your friend to find a photo and then check if anything she told you is true.' Charlotte entered her friend's name in the search bar and looked back at Scott wide-eyed.'

'Nooo!' she said incredulously.

'It looks like you may be having coffee with a princess – or with someone who looks remarkably like Princess Charlotte Marie Pomeline Casiraghi of Monaco. I think you need to do a little more research.'

'Blimey, Charlie! I'm coming too. This could be a fraud.'

'Or a wonderful scoop for *Hello*,' she retorted.

'That's not fair. I'm genuinely concerned about your safety and not just because your mother asked me to look out for you.' He paused thinking about what to say next. 'It's true that *Hello* would be delighted if I was able to interview the princess, but they don't know about this invitation and I have no intention of telling them. I'll tag along with you in the role of personal security detail only.'

'Thanks Mason. You can come along as my friend as well.' He smiled at her.

'Looks like I have two students for self-defence classes.'

'Too right,' said Mason. 'Can I look at your phone, Charlotte?' He stared at the image of the princess. 'You know, you two do look remarkably alike. Are you certain of your parentage?'

'Can't wait to hear Mum and Dad explain that one to me,' she replied with a mischievous grin. 'Yes, we noticed we looked a bit alike. It's what started us chatting in the first place. She had someone with her who called her *princess*, but I didn't think anything of it as that's what Dad calls me half the time. But that has definitely increased her TR score to 7.5.'

'Not high enough to avoid self-defence lesson. Over here you two.'

They practiced breaking from different holds for an hour on the yacht's main deck. At times, Charlotte failed to follow Scott's instructions without laughing. She felt awkward when he had his arms around her holding her close. She liked the feel of his body against hers and recognised that she was growing fond of him.

'That's the best I can do. Keep your wits about you. You're likely to be more intelligent than they are. Don't forget that.'

'Aye aye, captain,' she said, saluting. He smiled, rolling his eyes.

'Mate, you've got my number?' Mason gave him the thumbs up. 'OK. Have a good day and I look forward to hearing all about it. And can you message me when you're planning on being back. I'll make sure someone's at the gate to let you in.' They both nodded and waved goodbye as they ran down the gangplank and walked in the direction of the railway station where Charlotte had arranged to meet her new friend.

Mason spotted a silver BMW with darkened windows waiting at a traffic light to turn into Antibes railway station.

'If your friend is in that car, the TR score goes up by half a percentage point.' Charlotte punched him in the arm as she watched the car drive slowly towards them. A back window slid down and her friend from *Paris-Match* came into view.

'I see you've brought a friend along?'

'Part friend. Part bodyguard. There was a trust issue and I wasn't allowed to get into a car with a stranger.'

'Very sensible. I'm familiar with those issues. I've Gilles here for the same reason,' she said pointing to the driver. 'Hop in. My name's Charlotte. And yours?'

'Mason. Mason Murray.'

'Nice to meet you, Mason.'

'OK. So the TR score just increased another point,' Mason whispered. Charlotte gave him her sternest look as she put on her seatbelt.

'You both OK to come to Monaco for coffee? I have a lovely terrace.'

'That would be super.'

'Yes, we have time,' Mason chipped in. Charlotte subtlety practiced one of the elbow techniques Scott had just taught her, landing a devilish blow to his ribs. He grimaced and then grinned. 'Charlotte?' Both women answered yes. 'I think that we should come up with a naming convention so there's no confusion,' Mason suggested.

'You can call me Charlie, but don't tell Scott.'

'OK Charlie Girl.' He again received an elbow to the ribs.

'Who's Scott?' the princess asked, wondering what was going on between the two Australians sitting beside her.

'He's my best friend's brother. We bumped into him on Thursday on the pier after we collected the bottle.'

'Ah the bottle. You collected it. What was inside?'

'A letter of love. For my brother. It was beautiful. I was so moved. I don't think I'd ever really thought about how my brother's death affected them. I mean I've known about it all my life. But you don't really see your parents as people, do you, when you're a kid. I don't know. It was very moving.

The princess nodded and looked out the window lost in thought. Charlotte imagined that she was reflecting on her own losses, which she knew from her research included losing a father in an accident. The car continued to speed along the motorway with the occupants sitting in silence. Suddenly the princess spoke.

'And what of the sailor? Was he handsome?' The question surprised Charlotte.

'Very. And a wonderful kisser.'

'Kisser?' the princess asked. 'He certainly moves quickly.' They all laughed. 'What was his name?

'Jacques. Jacques Dessault.'

'Oh. He was on his father's yacht?'

'No. No, I don't think so. He was just a deckhand.'

'I see,' she murmured. She appeared about to say something else but hesitated. 'Yes. I must be mistaken.'

'Why did you think his father owned the yacht?'

'His last name is well known in France. A family of industrialists with many business interests. As I said, I'm sure I'm mistaken. And I also thought you had only just met? N'est-ce pas? Kissing?' The princess had again subtly shifted the conversation.

'We'd only just met for the first time on Thursday when he gave me the bottle. I think he kissed me because he got caught up in the moment. It was an emotional day.'

'I think he kissed you to avoid me getting a good photo of his face,' Mason interjected.

'You're just jealous and don't believe that in such a short time we could make a connection.'

'You'll be keeping in touch then?'

'Perhaps. We'll see,' Charlotte added feeling annoyed by Mason's cynicism. An awkward silence hung in the car for a moment and was then broken again by the princess.

'That's St Paul de Vence on the left there. It's a beautiful village full of artists. I always come away with at least one painting. I love the arts and like you, Charlie, I love fashion. I'll show you the beautiful dress I am wearing to the Rose Ball tonight. It's wonderful whimsy. I feel like I am from another era when I put it on.'

'Oh, I'd love that. It was so much fun at *Paris-Match* experimenting with different outfits. I felt like a different person each time I changed my dress.'

'I see that you changed your hair since Paris. I liked the purple streaks.'

'Well, they say that travel broadens your mind and I wanted for there to be some evidence that the trip had changed me, even if it was only symbolic.'

'And do you think it has?'

'Possibly. I think that I'm already more confident. Mason has been with me most of the time, but I think I could travel on my own and get myself out of bother if need be.'

'I'm sure you could. And Mason, what do you do when you are not acting as Charlie's chaperone?'

Mason hesitated.

'I'm a reporter at *Hello*.'

'I see. You're a member of the paparazzi?'

'Guilty. Kind of. A reporter more than a photographer and not always and definitely not now. You have my word. I'm only here as I promised Charlie's mum that I'd keep her safe. I'll not be taking any photos or reporting on anything that we discuss from this trip. Again, you have my word.'

'A man of honour. There are not enough of these in the world. I do wish that there were more *papps* who behaved with integrity. They are the bane of my life.'

'How do you deal with them?' Charlotte asked.

'Very carefully. They are wolves and can be deceptive. I understand that we are part of the same eco-system. They need a good photograph to earn a living and our fame can support many worthy causes as well as sell magazines. For example, the Rose Ball tonight is dedicated to raising funds for the foundation set up in my grandmother's name, The Princess Grace Foundation. It is considered the social event of the year in Monte Carlo and members of my extended family will attend in all our finery. So also do all the paparazzi. I'm surprised that *Hello* hasn't managed to get you a press pass.'

'Funds are a bit tight I imagine, so we focus our efforts in the UK.'

'I see,' she replied.

The car pulled up outside a long row of apartments which

were alternately painted light orange or yellow. Shutters on the outside windows were painted either grey or deep green and tiny terraces were framed by beautiful and intricate black ironwork. They would have looked perfect in any fairy tale, Charlotte thought. Gilles opened the door for the princess while Mason and Charlotte scrambled out the other side before realising that they should have waited for Gilles to open their door too. They walked through a beautiful reception area, formal lounge room and out on to a large terrace with a magnificent view of Monte Carlo and the Mediterranean.

'Wow,' Mason couldn't help his involuntary expression of delight.

'It's great, isn't it? I never tire of the view either.' The two Australians walked the full length of the terrace taking in the views from the craggy rocks to the tightly knit condominiums, the crowded port to the back of the palace perched on its own mighty, rocky plinth.

'Why do you live here and not in the palace?' Charlotte gave Mason an angry glare, thinking his question impertinent. Unfazed, the princess responded.

'My uncle Albert is the reigning monarch of the Principality of Monaco so the palace is his official residence. We are of course always welcome and there is plenty of room. My family will rendezvous there later this afternoon before the ball tonight. We all feel strongly about supporting The Princess Grace foundation and it's a great occasion to wear beautiful clothes.'

A maid appeared and the princess asked, 'would you like tea or coffee?' The maid noted their preferences and left a selection of sandwiches and macaroons on a beautifully decorated cake tower atop a large sideboard.

'Please take something and let's sit on the terrace.' The

princess's phone buzzed and she looked at it with consternation. 'Would you excuse me for a moment please?'

'Of course.' She left the room, leaving Charlotte and Mason alone.

'You know, you should interview the princess for your assignment on what makes a story go viral. I bet she'd have an interesting perspective.' Charlotte was annoyed and intrigued in equal measure by Mason's suggestion. Annoyed because she felt she was asking too much of her new friend and intrigued because she was certain that the princess would have a unique perspective. When the princess returned twenty minutes later, she was clearly agitated.

'You OK?' Charlotte asked.

'I'm sorry. I'm distracted.' She sat down and then stood up again and paced the room. Suddenly she stopped and looked at Charlotte.

'Can I help you?'

'Maybe. Just maybe. I have a problem. Or rather, my best friend has a problem. I want to help her, but I have the ball tonight.'

'Can we help your friend for you?' The princess looked at them both and nervously chewed her thumb nail.

'Do you speak Italian?'

'No. Sorry,' Charlotte replied. The princess looked out the window for a moment and then back again.

'Excuse me again for a moment.' The princess started dialling a number on her phone and walked out of the room.'

'Perhaps we should go. There's clearly something amiss,' Mason whispered.

'Let's see if we can help first. If not, I agree, we should leave.' They heard snatches of an animated conversation in

French from the next room. Fifteen minutes later the princess returned. She walked towards them tentatively.

'You may be able to help me.'

'Of course,' they responded in unison.

'My best friend's in trouble. She's hiding in the basement of a house in Milan because she is certain her fiancé has been kidnapped. The Italian police doubt her story and will do nothing for twenty-four hours and she is afraid the kidnappers will come for her. I want to go and bring her back here where she is under our protection, but of course I have the ball tonight.'

'Why would her fiancé have been kidnapped?'

'Gambling debts, I suspect. He owes money to a nasty Sicilian syndicate. She thinks he's been betrayed and doesn't know who to trust. Except for me. If Gilles and I leave now, we should be able to get there and back before the ball starts. If not, then things will be awkward. My absence will be noted and a story speculating why I'm not present will go viral. I need to avoid this. I also have obligations to be at the ball as many donors will be there and will expect to meet me. I also have a requirement for *the dress* to make an appearance. It has been leant by a major fashion house, who are also financially supporting the event. As a result, I have a request – a favour. Would you mind being my back up, Charlie? Would you be prepared to wear the dress until I arrive, so no one thinks anything is amiss?'

Charlotte's eyebrow shot upwards and a large grin rolled across her face. 'Of course,' she replied.

'I'm not so sure about this,' Mason chipped in.

'We'll get you a press pass so you can continue your role as chaperone. That way you can keep your promise to her mother.'

Mason's mind was suddenly buzzing with the opportunities available from being at the ball. 'And can I take photos like any normal member of the press?'

'Bien sûr. It would be suspicious if you did not.'

Mason smiled, thinking about how pleased Jane would be. Then he remembered his primary role was to look out for Charlotte.

'Surely people will spot her accent and know she's a fake, a substitute.'

'We'll say I have a sore throat which is why my voice sounds strange and why my participation in the event is limited. I will ask my Aunt Stephanie to stay close and ensure none of the guests approach you and speak in Italian. Most of the guests will be French-speaking so you will have no problem there. And we'll say you have to leave early because of your cold. Gilles can then drive you both back to Antibes. Do you think that would work?'

'Perfectly,' Charlotte announced without hesitation.

'I'm in, too,' Mason added, with a grin extending from ear to ear.

Ten minutes later Gilles had dropped the three of them at the front of a large door in a narrow street at the foot of the rock. There was a single guard who nodded at the princess before opening the door. Behind the door was a small courtyard leading to an elevator.

'This is the back entrance to the palace. Gilles can pick you up here later.' The elevator was sparkling and travelled smoothly to the interior of the palace. There was a bustle of activity inside. Staff nodded and curtseyed as the trio followed the princess into a room set aside for her family. 'This is the staging area. There is a team here to get you ready with hair, makeup and whatever else you need. Mason?'

'Yes?'

'I will arrange for you to be measured for a suit. Even the press have to be well presented at the ball.'

'Of course.' He raised his eyebrows while looking sheepishly across at Charlotte.

'Any questions?'

'We're fine. Go. Get your friend and get her back here. Hopefully we'll see you in a few hours and you can get back in time to wear *that dress* to the ball.' The princess leaned in and kissed them both and then ran back down the corridor to the elevator. Mason and Charlotte looked at each other and started laughing.

'You have my permission to pinch me, Mason. Later, not now. I'm in a dream and I'd like it to go on for just a little longer.'

'And long enough for me to get a few fabulous photos to dazzle Jane. What should we tell Scott about our expected arrival time?'

'Well, obviously the great news that you've been given a press pass for the Rose Ball. And as a result, you're not sure what time we'll get back. Probably around midnight.' Mason texted Scott the message. Moments later there was a reply.

'He's asking what you'll be doing while I'm at the ball?'

'Do you think he'd believe that I was working on my assignment?'

'Not for a nanosecond.'

'How about I'll be helping the princess in the background with stuff. That's true enough without giving the game away.'

'I'll try him.' Mason sent off the message and sat down

waiting for a reply. Moments later his phone pinged. He read the message and smiled.

'What'd he say?'

'That his TR rating for this explanation is 3 out of 10.' She laughed and sent Scott a smiley emoji. A few minutes later they were both invited to start getting ready for the ball.

17

PREPARATIONS FOR THE BALL

There was a gentle tap on the door.

'Oui?' Charlotte replied.

It was Mason. 'Your highness I've been told to leave the palace and make my way to the press enclosure at the ball. Is there anything more that you will be needing of me?'

Charlotte smiled at her friend. 'You do scrub up well, Mr Murray. Very impressive.' She took a photo on her phone of Mason in his black tuxedo with a press badge on a lanyard. 'If I don't see you at the ball, play nice with the other journalists and I'll meet you on the other side of the secret door just before midnight.'

'Agreed. I'm guessing that you've not heard anything from the princess?'

'No. Not yet. We're giving her another thirty minutes before I put on the dress. See you in an hour or so.'

Mason waved and followed a courtier outside to a waiting car. Charlotte looked at the photo on her phone and sent a message to Miranda.

Message to Miranda. *Your man scrubs up well. He's managed to wangle himself a press pass to the Rose Ball in Monaco. Thought you'd like this snap.*

From Miranda. *Thank you. He looks yummy. What are you doing?*

To Miranda. *Hanging around.*

Charlotte thought for a while about what message to send to her parents. Keep it simple she thought to herself.

Message to Mum and Dad.
Greetings from beautiful Monte Carlo. See attached snap taken from friend's terrace. Last day of sightseeing before I start the journey home tomorrow.

Message from Mum and Dad
Your friend has a lovely view from her apartment. You can tell us all about her when you get home. We hope that you've had a wonderful time and collected good information for your assignment. See you Tuesday. Love and hugs Mum and Dad

The assignment seemed so far away from her current world. Still she'd have to work on it tomorrow morning before they left for the airport to begin her long journey home. For now, she should note down a few thoughts for the reflective journal, which was due the same day as the assignment.

Reflective Journal – Saturday March 24

Apparently, a single photo can go viral and make you famous. We shall see.

Famous people and the members of the press sometimes have the same and at other times competing interests.

Famous people are real people with real lives who experience anxiety and loss – just like we normal folk.

It's amazing how a change of clothes can bring a change of perspective, a higher confidence and a new way to behave.

'Can I introduce myself?' Princess Stéphanie had quietly entered the room.

'How do you do,' Charlotte said automatically. She reached out her hand and then awkwardly curtseyed thinking that a handshake was probably not appropriate.

'I'm ...'

'The substitute. I know. Another hair-brained scheme from my niece. She was right though. You do look alike, although you are a younger version.' Another woman entered the room and regarded her carefully. Charlotte immediately identified her as Princess Caroline.

'Hello, Charlotte,' she said simply. Charlotte curtseyed again. 'I'm your mother. We kiss each other on the cheek. We don't curtsey. You'll give the game away if you do that again.' They all smiled.

'I've just received a text from Charlotte. She's collected

Anna and they left Milan thirty minutes ago. She won't be here for another two hours, so you will need to wear her dress and smile for the cameras.'

'Of course. That would be my pleasure.'

'I'll just go and brief the others.'

'Can you let me know who will know who I am?' Princess Caroline smiled. 'Of course. Your uncle and his wife, Prince Albert and Charlene. Your brother and sister. And of course, your boyfriend.'

'I have a boyfriend?'

'Indeed, a very-soon-to-be fiancé. I see that my daughter did not spend a lot of time briefing you.'

'A fiancé. Wow. I have a fiancé. Wouldn't my mother be surprised.' Charlotte started laughing and then stopped herself. Princess Caroline and Stéphanie were watching her and were equally amused.

'Anything else I should know?' The princesses looked at each other for a moment and then Princess Caroline gave her sister a knowing nod.'

'Don't drink tonight. The world does not yet know that my daughter is three months pregnant. When they find out, the media will not treat you kindly if they see that you have been consuming alcohol.'

'Of course. I will say I can't drink because of my cold.'

'Thank you.' There was a knock at the door. 'Marie is here to help you dress. Do you have any other questions?'

'What's my boyfriend's name?'

'Dimitri. He will be along to collect you shortly.'

'Thank you.'

The sisters left and Charlotte began her transformation.

18

THE FAIRY TALE

Charlotte kept staring at herself in the mirror. The transformation was amazing. She was wearing a long black dress with a large white ostrich feather wrap over one shoulder. Her hair had been pulled back in a tight roll and she carried a small black clutch bag. The makeup was minimalist, with scarlet lipstick and matching nail polish.

There was a cough. She turned to see a softly bearded guy with lovely eyes staring at her.

'You look lovely.'

'Thank you, Dimitri.' He offered his elbow to her and she sashayed over to him using the walk she had practiced in Paris.

'How lucky I would be to have two of you in my life.'

'One can but dream,' she quipped. He laughed. They joined the other family members who had congregated in the reception area. Prince Albert nodded towards her and Charlene winked. She was beginning to feel like she was a part of this royal community.

'You do very well,' Stéphanie remarked. They filed out to

a row of vintage cars that transported them a short distance to the Monte-Carlo sporting club. She exited the car and was overwhelmed by an explosion of camera flashes. She smiled into the brilliant light and took Dimitri's elbow again as they walked into the Salle des Etoiles. An orchestra was playing as they entered the ballroom. Nine hundred evening dress-clad guests stood and then clapped enthusiastically as they walked in and took their seats.

Charlotte looked around the room at the New York City Skyline decorations and was instantly transported back to *Paris-Match*'s offices where she had first met the princess. How far her life had moved in four days. The heady scent of the white and pink roses adorning the tables took her by surprise, transporting her back to her grandfather's home in Bangalow. She wondered what he might be doing now. Probably checking his cattle or having morning tea with Helen on the veranda. Her dreamy state was interrupted by a waiter offering her a champagne cocktail. She politely refused and scanned the room to see if she could spot Mason. It took a few minutes to identify him, as all the men were wearing near identical suits. She was delighted to see that he had been given a place at the end of one of the far tables. He saw her looking at him and he ever so slightly lifted his champagne glass. She smiled and turned her attention to the centre stage where raffle ticket winners were being announced. When this process was finished, an army of waiters served oysters and truffle flavoured lobster to all guests. Charlotte wasn't sure if she was meant to be eating oysters, given her 'delicate condition' and cast her eyes towards Stéphanie, who looked at her and grimaced. She sighed as she was hungry, not having eaten anything since they'd enjoyed morning tea on the terrace. Her thoughts flickered to the princess and she wondered if she'd arrived back safely with her friend. Dimitri had left to take a call and her 'mother', Caroline was talking with a well-known designer. The waiter returned with a small aubergine bake, which she gratefully ate, before nibbling on a bread role while waiting until the next course arrived. It was chicken and soft-shell crab tempura with rice. She looked at Stephanie who again shook her head. She pushed the plate aside as Dimitri returned. He sat down and whispered in her ear.

'They're back safe and sound.'

Charlotte smiled with relief. 'Wonderful news. Should I, should we return?'

'Shortly. After dessert there'll be a photo shoot and we should be able to slip out when that finishes.'

Dessert arrived including a trio of cheesecakes, a brownie, and a slice of pecan pie. Charlotte devoured hers and asked Dimitri if she could finish his as well. He smiled, patting her on the hand. A young girl approached the table.

'Photo time, sister.' Charlotte recognised the princess's half-sister Alexandra. She was wearing a fawn coloured drop-waisted dress with a satin skirt and had her hair pulled back in a ponytail. She was clearly enjoying the evening's charade. 'It's a pity our brother Andrea was unable to come tonight,' she remarked.

'Agree. It won't be a complete line up for the family photo with only you, Pierre, myself and mother of course.' Alexandra giggled and left to join her boyfriend. Charlotte wistfully watched her walk away, reflecting on how odd it felt to have a sister and two brothers. Tonight was certainly a first on many fronts. She looked around the ballroom at the dazzling dresses the women were wearing. They were a myriad of colours and textures while the men all looked like Michelin star waiters in their black suits and matching bow ties. She was curious to know what they were discussing. Dimitri touched her shoulder as he stood up, signalling that it was time to join the others. She could see many photographers waiting expectantly, Mason among them. The light bulbs started flashing as soon as she joined the rest of the royal family in front of the Manhattan skyline backdrop.

'Vous êtes magnifique ce soir,' one of the photographers called out.

'Merci,' she replied quietly remembering she was meant to have a heavy cold.

'Yes, indeed you are beautiful, your majesty,' Mason announced, trying to display a confidence that did not reflect how he was feeling.

'Thank you. And which magazine do you represent?'

'*Hello*. I come from *Hello*.'

'Please pass on my best wishes to your readers.' The other photographers looked on jealously and started competing to get her attention.

'Can we have a photo of you with Dimitri?' they called out. She nodded and Dimitri moved closer, putting his arm around her waist.

'We understand you're engaged? What do you say?' Charlotte looked at Dimitri for guidance on how to respond. He smiled, leant in and kissed her passionately. Charlotte's head was spinning. What was it with these men kissing her with no prior notice?

'That is what I say to you.' A ripple of laughter reverberated across the room. Dimitri took her hand and led her out. The paparazzi started whispering, assuming an engagement announcement was imminent.

'Ready to go?' Dimitri asked

'One moment,' she replied, texting Mason. They could see Gilles standing by the car. He was trying to keep away photographers who had camped outside in the hope of getting a unique photo.

'Princess! Over here,' they cried out. Charlotte waved and tried to smile as she scanned the crowd for Mason as the photographic flashes continued to explode. She was feeling anxious. Mason emerged at the edge of the press posse. Dimitri opened the car door for her and signalled for Gilles to let security know that it was OK for Mason to join them. Moments later the three of them were safely inside. Cries of disappointment could be heard from the paparazzi as they drove away.

'That escape was well executed. Wow, what a night,' Mason whispered to Charlotte. 'I've made some brilliant contacts.'

'And I hope you managed to take a photo or two.'

'A few. It's a lot harder taking photos as a member of a pack than when you're on your own. I may have consumed a few too many champagne cocktails which didn't help. And did you taste that truffle-flavoured lobster? My word. Out of this world.'

Charlotte thought about responding for a moment but chose to smile instead. Minutes later they were inside the palace and the real Princess Charlotte was cocooned within Dimitri's arms.

'Do not ever go away like that without telling me,' he scolded her between kisses.

'You would not have let me go if I'd asked,' she retorted.

'That is true. It was dangerous.'

'But I was successful. Anna is now safe, and I've managed to goad the DIA into investigating Gian-Paolo's disappearance.'

'So, you'll leave the investigative work to them.'

'If you say so,' she replied demurely. Neither Charlotte or Mason thought for a moment the Princess would comply.

'Do you feel like dancing?'

'Always.'

'Then get changed so we can get back to the ball and leave these good folk to go home.'

She kissed him on the cheek and reached out for Charlotte's hand. 'Come.'

Thirty minutes later the real Princess Charlotte was ready to attend the ball and the Australian pair were wearing their own clothes and ready to return to Antibes.

'Gilles will be waiting for you outside the gate. It is best you take the back door again.' The princess gave them both a big hug. The white feathers caused Mason to sneeze and they all laughed.

'There are no words adequate,' she began, 'thank you for being open to my crazy plan. You were wonderful by all accounts Charlie. I look forward to seeing the photos.'

'Speaking of photos,' Mason asked holding up his camera

'Yes?'

'May I take a photo of you and Dimitri? It would mean a great deal if I had one photo that was different to all the others captured tonight.'

'Why of course. And I'm sure the world will wonder why I have such a smile on my face.'

'That would be because you are so in love with me,' Dimitri offered. They all laughed as the princess snuggled up close to Dimitri. She was beaming and Mason quickly captured their smiling faces. Moments later the lift had closed and they were descending to the base of the rock below the castle.

'Did you know that tickets for the ball were eight hundred euros each? My oath. No wonder she didn't want to let anyone down.' A bell rang and the elevator doors opened into the small courtyard. It was cold so they both buttoned up their jackets.

'It's ten past twelve,' Charlotte observed looking at her phone. 'I wonder if Cinderella's carriage has turned into a pumpkin?'

'A bright orange BMW perhaps. Now that'd be worthy of a photo.' Mason opened the gate and they walked back into the real world. It was eerily quiet. 'I guess the guard knocks off at midnight.' He looked up the road and saw a silver BMW slowly approaching.

'Here come Gilles. No orange BMW though.'

'Bit of a relief really. Orange doesn't match what I'm wearing.' The car stopped a short distance from them and waited. Charlotte's eyes flickered across to Mason. It was odd that Gilles was not already out to open the door for them. Suddenly both doors opened and two men in black suits emerged from the driver and front passenger sides.

'Mason, my TR score is falling,' Charlotte whispered. Mason looked from one man to the other nervously.

'Where's Gilles?' he asked.

'He's hurt his hand, so I'm driving.' For a moment no one moved. The taller of the two men opened the back door and signalled for them to get in. 'You can ask Gilles yourself. He's here.' Mason walked slowly towards the car watching the two men carefully. He peered inside and was horrified to see Gilles bound and gagged.

'Run,' he yelled before he fell to the ground under a crushing blow to his forehead. Charlotte fled at Mason's cry.

The taller of the two men stopped her flight by grabbing her backpack. She turned and karate chopped him in the throat, poked him in the eyes and then thrust a knee between his legs, causing him to shout out in pain before rolling in a ball on the ground. He clearly hadn't been expecting this level of resistance. The other man thundered past him and grabbed her firmly. Charlotte started to scream and had a smelly rag thrust over her nose and mouth. She shook her head violently, before succumbing to the effects of the chloroform and collapsing to the ground. They carried her back to the car and dumped her in the trunk. The larger of the thugs kicked Mason who was still out cold. He groaned slightly. An envelope was placed under his head. It had a number with eight digits and a skull and cross bone symbol. The meaning was clear.

19

HANGOVER

Mason was shivering and his head hurt like nothing he had experienced before. He opened his eyes slowly and was confused by the darkness. He remembered what had happened and sat up quickly. Where was Charlotte? The wind caught the envelope that had been under his head and it started to dance merrily down the road. He rolled onto his feet and stumbled after it as fast as his throbbing head would allow. A deft stomp of his right foot stopped its flight. He could see that it was just an envelope and felt relieved until he turned it over. The light from his phone illuminated the numbers and, in that moment, his worst fears were realised. She'd been taken. A myriad of questions flooded his muddled head. Who had taken her and why? How long had he been lying on the road? Would the princess still be at the ball? His phone buzzed interrupting his efforts to make sense of the situation. A text message had arrived from Scott.

Ahoy party people. When should I expect you home? He took a deep breath and pressed the dial button.

'I'll be at the gate in two minutes,' came a sleepy reply.

'No mate. We're not at the gate. In fact, we're in a bit of trouble.'

'Go on.'

'She's gone.'

'What?'

'Someone's taken her. They think she's the princess.'

'What? Why would they think that?'

'Because she was the princess for a few hours.'

'Start talking, Murray. And quickly?'

Mason rapidly explained the situation to his friend.'

'Where are you now?'

'I don't know. Near the secret entrance to the palace.'

'What state was Charlotte in when they took her?

'I don't know?'

'Did she still have her phone?'

'Don't know. Wait a sec.' Mason looked at his Strava app. 'She's moving. She's on the water, on a boat travelling east.'

'Send me the link, go back inside and get them to call the national guard. And Mason –'

'Yeah?'

'It's not your fault. We'll get her back.'

Mason banged on the timber door for the fourth time. No response. He doubted anyone inside the palace could hear, but surely there must be security cameras somewhere. He assessed his options. Call the princess. But he didn't have her number and it seemed unlikely he'd be able to get through to her via the palace switchboard – if one was open at this time. The front entrance. He could get in there. But where was it? He switched on his phone and spoke to Siri, 'Palace Monaco.'

'The Prince's Palace of Monaco. Here you go,' the perky voice informed him. 'You are six hundred metres away. Turn right ...' Mason grinned slightly. He was not alone. He picked us his bag and followed the directions of his automated friend. With every step he was aware of where he'd hit the pavement and his pain and distress was compounded by the low battery warning signals his phone was emitting. Ten minutes later he walked tentatively up to the palace's front entrance. Two guards appeared.

'C'est la même mec,' one of the guards whispered to the other. They know me, Mason thought to himself. From the ball, or from the fight on the other side of the palace, he wondered.

'Je, je ...,' Mason's French suddenly failed him. 'I need to speak to Princess Charlotte. It's urgent.'

'You are paparazzi,' the whisperer responded.

'Well, no. I'm a reporter. But I'm also the princess's friend.'

'Then why don't you call her?'

'I've lost her number and my phone battery is dying.' The two offices looked at one another and raised their eyebrows.

'You have been drinking, sir?'

'I had a glass or two of champagne at the ball, but that's irrelevant.'

'It is clearly affecting your memory for telephone numbers.'

'Look. I never had her number. My friend did.'

'Then ask your friend.' The guards were beginning to enjoy themselves.

'I can't.'

'Why not?'

'I can't tell you.'

'And you also cannot tell us your business with the princess.'

'Exactly.'

'Monsieur. It is late, or rather it is early. Too early for this nonsense. Go home. Sleep off your champagne. And tomorrow ...'

'Tomorrow may be too late for my friend.'

'That is not our problem.'

'You leave me no choice but to go to the police. Princess Charlotte would have preferred I came to her first.'

'And why is that?'

'As I said before – I can't tell you.'

'So mysterious,' the guard cooed sarcastically.

'You leave me no choice. You will have to answer to the princess.'

The taller of the two guards, who had been watching the conversation with his colleague in silence suddenly spoke.

'D'accord. OK. OK. Viens avec moi. Come with me.' Startled and relieved Mason nodded. He didn't know why the guard had suddenly changed his mind.

'Thank you,' he replied meekly, following them into the palace and into a small room with a single sofa, and a table with jug of water and flowers. There was also a door which led to a bathroom.

'Go wash yourself up,' the guard directed. Mason turned on the bathroom light and was shocked at his reflection. Dark bruises on his forehead and cheeks were forming and blood had dribbled onto his cheeks from where his attacker had hit him. Splashing warm water on his face, he cringed in pain. When he emerged, he saw the door to the room was closed. He tested it. Locked tight. He was a prisoner. And his phone's battery was dead.

20

BAD DREAM

Charlotte rolled over and fluttered her eyes. It was dark but she could see a sliver of light under the door. She sniffed. The scent was unfamiliar. A smile crept across her face.

'Thank goodness,' she whispered. 'It was a dream. An awful and yet wonderful dream. I'm back on Scott's boat. Thank God. Must have been something I ate. Mind you, I didn't eat that much, or did I?' she thought, struggling to separate the dream from her memory of what happened. Someone murmured.

'Mason? That you?'

'Shhh,'

'What?'

'Shhhhhh.'

She didn't understand and tried to sit up. Something was wrong. It was as if she was still dreaming as she couldn't move her feet, her head hurt, she was thirsty and there was a terrible taste in her mouth. Approaching footsteps distracted her from the fog in her head.

'Scott?' she whispered. Instinctively she closed her eyes

as the room was flooded by light. Standing in front of her was one of the men from her nightmare.

'Hai dormito bene, principessa?' Confused, she glared at her kidnapper, unsure of what to say. 'You do not speak the language of your father?' he roared. Charlotte was shocked at his anger and suddenly remembered who he thought she was.'

'He died such a long time ago and I was so little.' Her response surprised him. He grunted, then turned to close the door. Glancing around the room she could see Gilles with his hands and feet tied and tape across his mouth in one corner, and a man of dark features and curly hair similarly restrained in another. Both had sustained multiple injuries.

'This is unacceptable,' she asserted with a new-found confidence. 'Release them immediately!'

'You are in no position to make demands your highness.'

'You do not need them now you have me. Let them go.'

'In time, you will all be released. Once we have received the appropriate compensation.'

'Which is ...?'

'Venti milioni di euro.'

'Twenty million euro. An ambitious sum. And what has my uncle Prince Albert said?

'We have left the message with your friend to deliver to the palace.'

'What, who, how did you do that?' she replied, confused.

'Your paparazzi friend. We gave him the message.'

'And how did he respond?'

'He was not awake at the time we gave it to him.'

Charlotte paused, trying to understand what he meant. A gnawing fear for Mason's safety bubbled inside her.

'I don't understand,' she said, feeling panic rising.

'He had a sore head so was sleeping. We left the message under his head.'

'That won't work,' she responded, looking at him carefully. 'They'll need proof of life. They'll insist on hearing my voice before committing to any payment. Where is my phone? I'll call Albert directly.'

'We are not fools. You will reveal our location.'

'I don't know my location, do I? I'll say only what you want me to say. You have my word. Get my phone.' He glared at her, clearly uncertain as to how to respond. Without another word he turned off the light, walked outside and locked the door again, bringing darkness. Charlotte listened to his departing footsteps and crawled over to Gilles. She felt awkward running her hands over his body but found his face and removed the tape from his mouth.

'I'm so sorry mademoiselle. They followed me and ambushed the car just before I turned the corner to collect you.'

'It's OK. How are you?'

'My arm is broken, but I'm alright. Gian-Paolo however, he is not so good.'

'He's Anna's Gian-Paolo?' She felt Gilles nod. 'What have they done to him?'

'He has been pounded. I think he has cracked ribs and a broken jaw. He sleeps and groans.'

Charlotte squinted in the darkness at the dishevelled man and assessed her options. Neither of the two men were in a position to overcome their kidnappers. The gentle rocking of the room and diesel fumes confirmed that they were on a boat. But where? Escape by water was the most likely way out. Approaching angry voices interrupted her thoughts. She gently replaced the tape over Gilles' mouth and crab-crawled back to her corner.

A tall, thin man entered the room behind the stocky, shorter assailant who had left the message under Mason's head. She recognised him now, from The Rose Ball. He'd been part of the crowd of paparazzi. She wondered how he had managed to get through security to pose as a photographer. The second man had a menacing demeanour and wore a floppy cap on his head. A cigarette dangled from his lips as he carefully observed her. He lifted the cap to scratch his head revealing a barbed wire tattoo circling his bald head twice.

'Your highness' he said, doing a theatrical courtesy. She knew that he was mocking her but all she could think about was how painful it would have been to acquire the gruesome artwork on his skull. He clearly had a high pain threshold.

'What is it that I can do for you, your highness?'

'Warm water, antiseptic and bandages, please. I need to attend to the damage inflicted on my friends.'

'You're in no position to make demands.'

'I know. You have all the cards with me as your key bargaining chip. You can afford to be generous and help me to limit the impact of their wounds.'

'And if I don't?'

'You know I have no power here. I'm relying on you to do the right thing.' Both men snickered as though it was the funniest thing they'd ever heard. Their laughter roused the sleeping man who groaned, rolled over and looked around the room in fear.

'Are you OK, Gian-Paolo?' Charlotte asked. He blinked and nodded, confused. She turned to her pudgy captor. 'What's your name?

'Federico.'

'Federico. Put the kettle on and make a pot of tea when

you collect the bandages please.' He looked at the taller man who stepped aside from the doorway to give him room to pass. The menacing one extinguished his cigarette on the door frame, letting the butt drop to the floor and pulled a cork and penknife out of his pocket. In what was clearly a well-practiced action, he began to carve the cork with the knife.

'And your name would be?'

'Shut up. I'm not as stupid as my little brother or as vulnerable to your mind games.'

'I apologise. This is a difficult situation for all of us.'

'Stop that.'

'What?'

'That thing you're doing, being all understanding. We have the power. Not you. You are OUR prisoner. You family will meet OUR demands, or they will never see you again.' Charlotte's thoughts suddenly flickered across the ocean to her mother and father. They had no idea where she was. They'd be furious. They'd be terrified. They were probably planning her first meal for after they picked her up from the airport. She smiled at the thought of how excited they would be and then remembered her reality. She had to get out of here. She had to get home.

PRISONER

ederico returned with bandages and a bucket of warm water. He placed it in the middle of the room. 'Thank you. Antiseptic?' He shook his head.

'And the tea?' He grunted and stormed out, slamming the door hard.

Charlotte quickly moved over to Gilles and started gently washing the blood off his face.

'Do you have any idea where we are?' she whispered.

'We travelled for about an hour, so we could be anywhere from San Remo to Cannes. I doubt we are far from land.'

'Why do you think that?'

'Because they will need to select a ransom point which is easily accessible and has cover.'

Charlotte considered what this meant.

'How many others are on board?'

'Not sure. I can hear a television and voices. Maybe another two, perhaps three.'

'Do you think you could swim?'

'Non. Ce n'est pas possible. You go. Vas'y. I stay with Gian-Paolo.' At that moment the other captive groaned. Charlotte shuffled over to the semi-conscious Italian.'

'Gian-Paolo. How can I help you be comfortable?' His eyes fluttered open and he looked at her in distress.

'Sono così dispiaciuto. I'm so sorry.' Tears streamed down his cheeks.

'Shhhh,' she replied as she gently wiped the tears and grime off his face. They could hear an argument upstairs followed by heavy footsteps. Both men were coming back and coming quickly.

Charlotte was surprised to see a welt on Federico's cheek. Their other captor was in a foul mood, fidgeting with his penknife.

'You need to call your uncle and let him know where to drop off the money. It needs to be delivered to these coordinates or you will,' he paused, 'no longer be able to *take tea together*.' He passed a piece of paper and then threw a black phone at her. It bounced from her lap on to the floor. She picked it up and looked hesitatingly back towards them.

'I don't know his number off by heart. It's stored on my phone.' The brothers looked at each other and back at Charlotte suspiciously.

'You're lying!'

'Don't you have your family's numbers stored as favourites? Where's my backpack? My phone's inside. Get it and I'll make that call.'

'Carlo?'

'Non dite il mio nome,' the taller captor yelled, clearly furious his name had been revealed.

'Devo ...?' Carlo swept his hand to the door and Federico went scurrying out, returning moments later with her backpack. The phone was quickly retrieved, and Carlo tried unsuccessfully to turn the phone on.

'It needs my thumb for validation.'

Carlo growled and then held the phone up, keeping a firm hold of it. She nodded, indicating that the thumb validation was successful.

'Where's his number?'

'We use nicknames. His is Mason.' Carlo stared into her eyes, looking for signs she was lying. He did not trust her.

'Don't believe you. Why Mason?'

Charlotte's mind performed mental gymnastics.

'It's a complicated story that will mean nothing to you if you've not watched old American movies. My grandmother gave Albert the nickname, after the indomitable detective, Perry Mason. She loved his capacity to solve problems.' The scrawny Italian scratched the stubble on his chin while he assessed the story. He looked at his watch and growled again.

'This. You say this. And only this,' he yelled while holding up a scruffy piece of paper. Charlotte nodded. Carlo pressed Mason's number and passed the phone to her. It automatically went to message bank and Charlotte groaned.

'Voicemail,' she whispered. He waved his hand indicating that she should leave the message anyway.

Albert. Twenty million Euros in unmarked bills is demanded for my safe release. Do not attempt rescue. Do not call the police. Drop the money at the following coordinates by 6:00am Sunday 26 March Or you will never see me again.43.5050 degrees North, 7.0470 degrees East

·   ·   ·

She hung up.

'Perhaps he's asleep. What's the time?'

'Never you mind.'

'My mother may be awake. Can I call her?' Carlo again regarded her carefully.

'And her nickname?'

'C2.' She passed him the phone.

'And C stands for?'

'It's her name, silly. C for Caroline. She's annoyed when I call her Caroline, so I call her 'C2' as both our names start with C.'

He searched her phone directory and pressed C2 before passing her the phone. The call was automatically switched again to message bank. Charlotte shook her head and whispered, 'Message bank.' Carlo gritted his teeth, snarled and started pacing the room.

'Maman. C'est moi. I've left the following message with Uncle Albert.' Charlotte repeated the message given to Mason, rang off, noting the time and the flashing light of the Strava APP, and passed the phone back to Carlo in a bid to gain his trust. 'I expect you'll get a call back very soon.' He looked at her face carefully again trying to identify any hint of deception. Ten seconds of awkward staring passed before Charlotte broke the silence.

'Now I've helped you. Help us. Tea for my friends. Now. Please,' Charlotte ordered. She hardly recognised herself. Carlo cast his eyes across at Gian-Paolo and Gilles sitting despondently in the corner and signalled to Federico to check their bindings. Federico roughly checked both men and the ropes that were restraining their feet and hands. Satisfied the men were contained, they left, locking the door behind them but leaving the light on. Charlotte waited until she could no longer hear retreating footsteps. She moved closer to Gilles and spoke softly.

'We could be found soon, so you need to prepare yourself. It may be chaotic when the rescue starts. Do you think you could barricade the door?'

'Peut-être,' he replied softly.

'What else do you know about the layout of the boat?'

'Very little, unfortunately. I was blindfolded until I was here. However, ...' He quickly explained what he assumed about the structure of the boat. Charlotte put her fingers to her lips, hearing Federico's distinctive shuffling footsteps outside. The clank of a metal tray was heard moments before the key turned in the lock. Federico placed the tray on the floor in the centre of the room and retreated, once again locking the door. On the tray sat a silver pot of coffee and half a baguette. She poured Gilles a cup and held it to his mouth.

'Merci,' he whispered. She passed him a chunk of break and poured another cup, moving over to the semi-conscious Italian.

'Gian-Paolo. Would you like coffee? Something to eat?' He moved his head very slightly.

'Si.' She gave him bread and coffee and examined her surroundings. There were no windows and the walls were bare except for a few hooks for storing ropes and carrying life vests. She wondered if she was being overly optimistic in thinking Mason would have already rallied a rescue team. Why hadn't he answered the phone? The last time she saw him he was telling her to run. What had happened to him? Was he still lying unconscious on the ground outside the palace? Perhaps he'd been badly injured?

Gian-Paolo started groaning and it was obvious from the

way his body was rocking that he was going to vomit. Charlotte grabbed a bucket from the corner of the room and held it against his chest. Moments later the contents of his stomach were evacuated, and he lay back against the wall, moaning. She washed his face and put her hand to his forehead, confirming a fever. What could she do? Her thoughts were interrupted by the sound of the key in the door. Federico peeked in and moved to collect the coffee pot. He sniffed the air, very aware of the rancid smell of vomit.

'I've been sick,' Charlotte suddenly offered. 'Can I wash out this bucket?'

'No.'

'Can you do it then?' She thrust the bucket towards him and his face screwed up in disgust at the stench. He stared at her considering his options. 'I'm pregnant.' This announcement startled him. 'Can I come onto the deck? Fresh air will help.' Unsure of what to do, he said nothing, grabbed the bucket from her and locked the door as he left. Gilles and Charlotte looked at each other as they listened to the bucket being filled with water and emptied in a nearby toilet. Federico went upstairs and they could hear animated voices. Ten minutes later Carlo and Federico came back. Carlo had a smile on his face.

'So, we have four prisoners? Basta. We should increase our demands.' Charlotte starting rocking slowly and put her hand to her mouth.

'The bucket,' she whispered. Federico passed it over and she continued for a moment with her faux pre-vomit movements before stopping. 'It's passed.' She breathed in deeply and exhaled slowly. 'I beg of you. Can I have a few moments of fresh air?'

'Solo cinque minuti,' Carlo replied. She was going to be given five minutes. She started to think about what information would be key in the event of a rescue. For effect she groaned and put up her hand indicating that she needed help to get off the floor. Carlo nudged Federico, who knelt down beside her, untied the ropes binding her feet and put his arms around her to help her stand. The door was locked behind them and they climbed a narrow staircase to a dining and seating area. There was a television playing in the corner and a steaming cup of coffee revealed another person's presence nearby. Charlotte noted a second narrower passageway near the television. The other person or persons must be down the other end of the boat. They climbed a second smaller staircase to the upper deck. The cold, fresh air hit her face with full force reviving her spirits. While it was still dark there was a shimmer of light from a half moon. And there was something else. She could smell eucalyptus.

'Siedi là. Sit there,' Carlo commanded, pointing at a small bench. She obediently sat taking in her surroundings. 'Corda,' Carlo yelled at his brother. Federico thundered downstairs returning moments later with rope. Charlotte's spirits sank as Federico bound her legs together. She knew she had to keep her arms free, so again pretended to be on the verge of throwing up.

'Bucket?' she asked meekly. Without reference to his brother, Federico descended and returned with the bucket. She wrapped her arms around its rim and thrust her head inside, gently rocking. Carlo tutted in disgust. In her weakened condition she did not appear to be a threat and the need to bind her arms diminished. A shout from the dining room caught their attention and they could hear the volume on the television being turned up. The sounds of an orchestra were familiar to Charlotte as it was the piece being played when the royal family had arrived at the Rose Ball.

One of the television channels was probably featuring high-lights. Her captors descended leaving Charlotte alone. She anxiously surveyed her surroundings. There were a dozen small boats anchored about five hundred metres away. If she called out, she knew that she would be heard by her captors and immediately taken back downstairs to the others. She turned her head in the direction of the scent of the euca-lyptus trees and wondered if they were anchored near the islands she had seen from the hilltop in Cannes. Her mind flickered to Mason and Scott and she wondered where they were. With the moonlight on the water a half-moon providing a little light, she thought she could see trees sway-ing. Distances were hard to measure, but the trees were probably two hundred metres away. She could swim that distance easily – if her feet weren't tied together. She consid-ered her options: stay where she was and wait to be rescued; call out to the nearby boat and hope that someone heard her; swim to shore and raise the alarm. A tiny flickering light from the trees caught her attention.

'Cooee,' came a bird-like call. That had to be Scott. Federico had heard the cry as well and ascended the stairs. Charlotte stuck her head in the bucket and groaned loudly.

'Oooee,' she creaked and then burped. He looked around slowly and, satisfied the prisoner was still incapaci-tated, returned to the television. A small flashing light was now visible in the water, moving slowly towards the boat. The music on the television below had changed to a slow waltz and there was a French commentator making observa-tions. The music was not a piece she recognised, and she heard snatches of discussion about what Princess Charlotte was wearing and if she was engaged to Dimitri. An animated Italian discussion had started below, drowning out the French commentary. She listened hard, trying to understand what they were saying. Suddenly she realised that the footage they were watching may have been taken after the real Princess Charlotte had returned to the ball. Her captors were confused, discussing the timing around when she had been taken. Charlotte suspected that it would only be moments before they returned to the upper deck to interrogate her. The least-worst option was now clear, so she shuffled to the railing and slipped her legs, still constrained by the ropes, over the railing and dropped into the chilly Mediterranean Sea.

22

A RUDE AWAKENING

Mason woke with a start. His neck was aching and he wasn't sure if the pain was from his attackers last night or from having fallen asleep in the chair. Someone was unlocking the door. He looked at his watch. 12:30. Couldn't be. It must have been damaged in his fall. How many hours had he been asleep? Charlotte? Where was Charlotte now? Two guards walked into the room followed by a distraught Princess Charlotte.

'I'm so, so sorry,' she spluttered. 'I'd no idea you'd been contained. They didn't want to wake me. Gilles has disappeared too. I've just listened to Charlotte's message and called Albert. This is horrible. Did she call you?

'I don't know, my phone's dead. Do you have a cable or charger? It's urgent. If she still has her phone with her, we'll know where she is.'

The princess issued instructions to one of the guards. As he left, Prince Albert and Dimitri rushed into the room. Dimitri put his arms around Charlotte and pulled her close.

'They think they have you. At least that should keep her safe.'

'Are you OK?' Albert asked, placing his hand gently on Mason's arm and looking at his black eye. Mason shrugged, momentarily lost for words.

'Let me listen to the message?' Albert directed at his niece. The princess passed the phone. He listened intently and then looked at Mason.

'I didn't get a call, and this message was intended for my sister,' he said looking at his niece. 'It's clear they still think they have a royal captive. Tell us what happened.'

Mason described what had transpired outside the secret door the previous night and handed the prince the envelope that had been placed under his head. The prince examined it carefully, holding it up to the light by the tips of his fingers.

'Forensics,' he called out, and one of his aids came and placed the message in a plastic bag before whisking it away for analysis.

'They have Gilles too. He will look after your friend.'

'I don't think so. He wasn't in a state where he was capable of looking after anyone.' Princess Charlotte's hand flew to cover her face and she leant back into her fiancé's arms. She then took a deep breath and attempted to shake away her fear.

'We have the coordinates for the drop off. We can give them the money and get them all safely back.'

'We have a protocol for situations of this sort, Charlotte. You know that. And clearly we do not want the world to know.'

'What do we do next?' Mason asked. Albert turned to the open door and clicked his fingers. Two uniformed guards appeared with computers and moments later another guard entered with a selection of charging devices.

Mason connected his phone and the battery light started beating like a small heart.

'I can see her phone signal,' he cried excitedly, showing his Strava screen to the prince and princess.

'They are hiding among the Iles de Lerins,' Albert declared, taking the phone from Mason for closer examination. 'And I am fairly sure that those coordinates for the ransom drop-off are on Saint Honorat.' The guard standing beside him nodded, pointing at the location on his device. 'How long ago did they call?

Princess Charlotte looked at her phone. 'Three hours.'

'They'll be getting anxious as they haven't heard from us.'

Mason suddenly remembered that he hadn't spoken to Scott.

'Phone, please,' he said to the prince. His eyebrows shot up as he listened to the automated message bank. There were ten missed calls and four messages.

Message 1: *Where are you, mate? Call me.*

Message 2: *You OK? Genuinely nervous now. Did you get into the palace? Call me.*

Message 3: *I know where she is. I'm on my way. Call me.*

Message 4: *Albert. Twenty million Euros in unmarked bills is demanded for my safe release. Do not attempt rescue. Do not call the police. Drop the money at the following coordinates by 6:00am Sunday 26 March or you will never see me again. 43.5050 degrees North, 7.0470 degrees East*

Mason immediately called Scott back. Voicemail. He groaned.

Mate, it's me. Got your messages. Sorry I've been incapac-itated. He involuntarily glared at the princess. '*We've heard from the kidnappers. They've warned us not to attempt rescue. I repeat DO NOT ATTEMPT RESCUE. Call me.*

Mason passed the phone back to Prince Albert.

'We need to move quickly. I don't know where Scott is, but he's on his way to break her out. And she's called me pretending to be calling you. We need to call back to confirm to her kidnappers that we're acceding to their demands. It should ensure her well-being.'

'Agreed,' the Prince nodded as he took Mason's phone back from him.

The phone rang four times before Carlo answered.

'You will meet our demands?'

'Yes, of course,' the prince replied. 'As soon as we have all three prisoners in our care you will get your money.'

'No. Money first and then we will release the prisoners.'

'Not acceptable.'

'I don't care,' Carlo screamed and then hung up. Everyone in the room looked at each other anxiously.

'Sir?' the head of security asked the prince. He nodded and the security team ran out the door.

23

AN HOUR EARLIER

Scott woke the second officer, apologised and explained that he was passing him command of the yacht and he'd be borrowing the small dinghy to collect a friend who 'needed to be rescued'. The ambiguous way the message was delivered gave the impression that a friend was drunk and had found themselves stranded on a yacht. This was a common occurrence on the super yachts moored principally for partying purposes on the Côte d'Azur. He packed medical equipment, warm clothes and a blanket into a backpack and placed it on the bottom of the dinghy moored to the yacht. He checked the Strava APP and was pleased to see that the boat with Charlotte's phone hadn't moved. He called Mason again and was frustrated when his call immediately diverted to voicemail. Where was he? He didn't leave another message. He untied the boat and quietly chugged out of the port of Antibes. It was a clear, still night and he was pleased there was half a moon providing light.

Thirty minutes later he steered the boat into a rocky inlet on the north side of the island of Sainte-Marguerite.

He tied the boat to a pine tree bent out over the water, slung on his backpack and clambered over the rocks and gnarly roots. He ran as quietly as he could through the forest to a point six hundred metres away, from where he could view the boat. There were lights on in a room in the middle of the vessel. Through binoculars he could see three men drinking coffee. There was no sign of Charlotte. He checked the Strava APP to confirm the location of her phone. It was still on the boat, and in all likelihood, Charlotte was too.

Scott reviewed his options. He knew that he could swim out to the boat and climb aboard undetected, but it would be difficult to get below without one of the thugs spotting him. Still, if he was captured, he'd be with Charlotte and better able to plan an escape. He secured his diver's knife around his calf, put on his wetsuit and looked through the binoculars one last time. There were now people on the upper deck. He focussed carefully and was relieved to see that Charlotte was one of them. 'Good girl,' he whispered. Moments later the men left her alone and Scott called out the familiar Australian *cooeee* call sign. Charlotte's head cocked. She'd heard him. But so also had one of the captors who'd come back up on deck to investigate. He could see Charlotte throwing up into a bucket – or was she just pretending? He shoved the binoculars into his backpack, hid it behind a rock, and crab-crawled down to the water's edge. He carried a tiny flashlight in his mouth. As he entered the chilly, dark water, he could hear his phone vibrating in his backpack. It was too late to go back for it now, as someone had just slipped overboard.

24

OVERBOARD

Aargh. The water was dark and icy. Far colder than she'd expected. Charlotte resisted the temptation to shoot for the surface and to fill her lungs with air, knowing that she had to be quiet and to put as much distance as she could between the boat and herself. Her clothes, full of water, made it hard to move easily and her legs were still constrained by the ropes. Instinctively, she started swimming like a mermaid, a method she'd spent hours practicing as a child. She longed for air, but knew she had to swim as far from the boat as she could on one breath. Thirty seconds later she emerged, fifty metres away from the boat. She looked back and was pleased to see that her disappearance had not yet been discovered. She inhaled deeply and ducked deep under the water, crawling her way forward in the direction of the light. As she emerged for air a second time a familiar voice whispered.

'Fancy meeting you here.' It was ludicrous to smile, but she was just so happy to see Scott. She wrapped her arms around him and caught her breath.

'You OK?'

She nodded. 'It's lucky I'm the daughter of a mermaid as my feet are tied together.'

'Impressive,' he responded, 'Let's get you to shore and I'll set you free.' They both took a deep breath and swam another thirty metres underwater, emerging to a moonscape of craggy rocks. The ropes binding Charlotte's legs caught on the rocks' jagged edges, ripping her jeans and deeply slicing her left leg. She swallowed a mouthful of seawater as she cried out in pain. Her scream caught the attention of her captors, who started sweeping the sea with torches. They'd been discovered. Scott helped her to stand up. She winced with the pain and her teeth started slamming against each other from the cold. He scooped her up and carried her into the forest, gently placing her on a small boulder. He cut the ropes binding her legs together and extracted dry clothes from his backpack. Their hearts were beating faster now as a small motorboat was pushing off from the yacht. Charlotte struggled to pull her soaking sweater over her head and Scott helped, tugging at the reluctant garment which was clinging to her body. He replaced it with a long-sleeved shirt and jacket. The small boat pulled up on the shore fifty metres away and Charlotte could see Federico and Carlo wading ashore. There was no time left to run. They had to hide.

A hollow behind a nearby rock provided a convenient hiding place. Scott pulled Charlotte close and covered them both with the blanket. Terrified, she took a slow deep breath and listened carefully for approaching footsteps. The men were not talking, clearly aware they might be heard, but the prevalence of dry twigs made their steps highly audible. They followed a searching pattern of five or six steps, stop and search with flashlight, repeat. The brothers continued this way together for fifteen minutes and then set off in opposite directions along the shoreline. It was quiet but Scott and Charlotte dared not move. Scott was assessing their options. He could easily make it to the boat in ten minutes, but Charlotte was injured and would need to be carried. Alternately he could leave her, run to get the boat and come back. But they might find her while he was gone and take her prisoner again. The best option was to stay put. For now.

Time passed slowly. Charlotte felt warm and safe in Scott's arms and started to drift off to sleep. Moments later they heard footsteps approaching, but they passed their hiding place and moved down to the water's edge. The outboard motor sprung to life and the sound diminished as it headed back to the yacht.

'How many people do you think got into that boat?' Scott whispered in her ear.

'Don't know. At least one. Maybe two.'

'I'm not sure either. Maybe one of them is hiding and waiting for us to reveal ourselves.'

'It's possible. But if there's only one, we have a better chance of evading capture.'

'I've never been good at waiting.'

'Me either. Let's make a run for it.' He carefully pulled the blanket off, rolled on to his haunches and peered over the rock. There was only the sound of wind through the trees and the gentle lapping of water against the rocks. Looking out to the yacht he realized that there was a risk the boat would return with a larger search party, particularly as the morning light was now only an hour or so away.

'Let's go.' He reached down and helped Charlotte to gingerly stand. She grimaced from the pain, but nodded to let him know she was OK. He swung the backpack on to his shoulders and they stepped out onto the narrow path. Charlotte walked as quickly as the pain would allow.

'Nearly there,' Scott whispered. As they came around the corner to a small inlet Scott hissed. 'Those bastards. They've taken the dinghy. That was why we only heard one set of footsteps.'

'Shhh,' Charlotte whispered, pointing further along the path. They could hear the unmistakeable whir of a line being cast into the water and see a shadow of someone sitting on a rock. 'I think it's a woman.' Scott shook his head.

'Why would you wear a dress fishing? It's a monk. There are a few at the monastery on St Honorat.'

'Maybe the fishing's better here?' They both watched the person continue to throw their line out to sea, careful not to move.

'We can't stay here, and they look settled. I wonder if they have a boat? They had to get here somehow.'

'What's your TR score?' Charlotte whispered. He laughed.

'Six, maybe seven.'

'Agreed. Let's risk it.' Charlotte took a step in the direction of the fisherman and called out. 'Monsieur, nous avons besoin d'aide. Can you help us?' Startled, the fisherman turned around.

'Mon Dieu. Why of course.'

'We came for a little picnic, drank too much wine, and while we were,' she hesitated, 'sleeping, someone borrowed our boat.' The monk laughed, clearly amused by the thought of two young lovers having a romantic tryst.'

'Un moment.' The monk reeled in his line and slid off his rock. Scott and Charlotte sighed with relief.

'I'm going to call Mason, and then look at your leg.'

'Non, monsieur. Not if you want to avoid another injury.' Scott turned to see a pistol pointed at Charlotte's head.

25

OPERATION CENTRALE

Screens flashed and phones rang incessantly in the command headquarters for 'Island Sweep'. It felt surreal, and Mason watched with fascination. His Strava App still revealed Charlotte's phone to be sitting on a vessel among the Iles de Lerins. A small contingent from a private military force were ready to extract 'the princess', her driver and possibly Gian-Paolo Romano. Another team was preparing for the money drop. Timing was critical. A thousand thoughts ran through his mind:

Was Charlotte OK?
Was she frightened?
Where the hell was Scott?
How will I explain this situation to her parents?

He felt guilty for wishing he could write a story about the rescue.

I'd be a hero at Hello.

Seemed unlikely they'd catch the last plane back to
London that day.
Facing Jane would be the least of my worries.
Losing my job and having to go back to Australia – not
so bad.

'Ready for the call.' The commander of the operation addressed Albert and passed him Mason's phone to make the call. It rang suddenly. Albert looked at the caller and passed the phone to Mason. It was Miranda calling on WhatsApp.

'Hey Miranda. Lovely to chat, but I'm kind of busy.' Mason gave the prince a look of helplessness. 'No. No. Charlotte's not with me. She's kind of tied up and I'm expecting an important work call. Gotta go.' He cut Miranda off and passed the phone back to the prince. He called Charlotte's number.

'This is Albert Grimaldi. A small boat with one passenger and a large bag will arrive on the island in five minutes. They will drop the money only after I have received confirmation my niece is alive and free. I repeat. I must have confirmation of life NOW!' The receiver hung up without uttering a word. They looked nervously at each other.

'Hold your positions,' the commander relayed into a communications device. Prince Albert scratched his chin nervously while Princess Charlotte stepped closer to Mason and put her hand on his shoulder. He looked at the electronic clock on the control board. 5:55. Three minutes passed. There was nothing else they could do but wait.

26

FORT ROYAL

Scott carried Charlotte up a steep incline into a heavily wooded area of the forest. The monk's gun was ever present against his spine. There was a small clearing with a camera on a tripod. The easterly wall of Fort Royal could be seen through the vegetation.

'What's this?' he demanded as the monk handcuffed him to a tree.

'Confirmation. We've been asked to prove the princess is alive before the money is dropped.'

Charlotte was handcuffed to another tree three metres away from Scott. Her leg was aching, and her wet jeans were irritating her wound. She let herself succumb to feelings of helplessness and started crying.

'No crying please, Chiquita. You're on candid camera.' Startled, they looked up at the camera with the tiny red light and watched their captor slip away back to the water's edge. It was still dark, and Charlotte wondered if anyone watching the video would be able to determine who she was.

'Help,' she screamed at the top of her voice. 'Aidez-nous s'il-vous-plaît.'

'Shhh,' Scott responded. 'Listen.' There was a loud, juddery sound approaching at speed.

Mason's phone began to ring.

'Incoming transmission,' the commander cried. 'Switching through to all screens.' A grainy image appeared of a wooded forest. There appeared to be someone handcuffed to a tree. 'Satellite images please.' The satellite image zoomed in to the spot at a startling speed. 'It's the target. Confirm money drop. Repeat confirm money drop. Action Operation Island Sweep NOW. Go. Go. Go.'

'You beauty,' Mason cried out with relief and hugged the princess, who was momentarily taken back. 'Sorry ma'am, I mean your majesty.'

'No worries,' she replied with a smile. 'We're nearly there. Come. Let's go to the collection point.'

'One moment.' Mason approached the commander of the operation. 'May I? My phone?' A quick nod and Mason collected his phone and once again dialled Scott. Voicemail. 'Mate, we've found her. Search and rescue are on the way. Where the hell are you?

Moments later a helicopter swooped overhead, causing leaves to drop like confetti and drowning out the sound of Scott's phone ringing. If he'd heard it, he wouldn't have been able to answer it anyway, as it was in his backpack more than ten metres away behind a rock.

'That might be the cavalry, or it might be your captors collecting their ransom.'

Two more helicopters swooped overhead again shaking the leaves from the trees. In the early morning light Charlotte could see they were larger and of a military style compared to the smaller one which had passed by moments before. Thundering footsteps could be heard through the trees and three black-clad figures raced towards them with lights that momentarily blinded them both. One man stood guard over them while the other two circled the area checking for enemy combatants. A light was shone directly in Charlotte's face.

'You're not the princess?' came a slightly accusatory tone from a distinctly British accent. Charlotte was weary, overwhelmed and beginning to feel a little weak from the loss of blood.

'No. I'm not the princess. I'm the substitute.' The tall figure standing over her pointed the light away from her face and took off his balaclava.

'I'm familiar with that condition,' he said with a broad smile. His ginger beard was unmistakable and Charlotte started laughing.

'Delighted to make your acquaintance. My name's Charlotte. Charlotte Wyatt.'

'And mine is Harry, Harry Windsor, but you know that already.'

Charlotte smiled and rattled the handcuffs. 'Can you please release me?'

He looked at the cuffs and then saw her bloodied jeans. 'I need a medic. Urgently,' he relayed into his device. He turned to Scott. 'You OK?' Scott responded with an OK sign and then pointed at his handcuffs. Harry smiled and used a piece of metal to release them both. He then gave them water and muesli bars. A tall woman with a large backpack came crashing through the trees as the early morning light began to reveal the beauty of the forest. Charlotte stared at the wall of Fort Royal that was now easy to see through the trees.

'Easier to break you free from a tree than if you were locked up in there,' Harry observed. The woman introduced herself and examined Charlotte's injury. Her leg was cleaned, and a local anaesthetic administered prior to the suturing of her wounds.

'There'll be a scar I'm afraid.'

'That's OK. All my family have scars. Not all of them are visible though.' She glanced at Harry who was watching her carefully.

'When was the last time you had a tetanus shot?' the doctor interrupted. Charlotte shrugged her shoulders. 'I'll take that as a *not recently.*'

'Ouch,' she cried out as the needle pricked her arm. Then she remembered. 'The boat! Gilles and Gian-Paolo are prisoners in the hold.'

'We know. We've been tracking the boat and ...' Harry's communication device suddenly crackled.

'Yes, sir. Both safe and in reasonable spirits. One requiring medical evacuation. Hmmm. Is Island Sweep completed?' Charlotte strained to hear what the voice on the other end was telling her princely rescuer. 'Roger that.' He reattached his device to a dog clip on his waist band. 'Two men have been liberated and are on the way to receiving specialised medical care.'

'And that is where you should be going now,' the doctor advised.

'No. Can't. Gotta plane to catch. Gotta get home.'

'That would be a little dangerous, in my opinion,' she replied sternly.

'I'm comfortable with dangerous.'

'You need rest and to keep that leg elevated.'

'I can do that. And I promise to get my leg examined again as soon as I can.' The doctor shrugged her shoulders and signalled to the men. They approached and unpacked a stretcher.

'And you? How are you?' the doctor asked directing her attention at Scott.

'I'm right.' The doctor smiled.

'Lucky, I understand Australian.'

'Found this, sir,' came a shout from one of the other paratroopers holding up a backpack.

'That's mine,' Scott called out. He rifled through the damp bag and found his phone, a red light flashing. Twenty percent battery life remained. He called Mason.

'Mate. Where've you been? Mason yelled into the phone.

'Hold up. I could say the same thing to you?'

'I was a bit tied up.'

'And so was I. I'm with Charlotte.'

'Wonderful. How is she?' At that moment he could hear Charlotte and Harry laughing.

'She's in fine spirits with a bit of leg damage.'

'What? What does that mean?' Scott's phone started beeping as the battery level reached fifteen percent.

'Outta battery. Get the bags and we'll meet you at the airport. Sorry, bye.' Scott shoved the phone in his pocket, hoisted his backpack over his shoulder and walked up the incline to where Charlotte was deeply engrossed in whatever Harry was telling her.

'... it was as simple as that really. When a friend reaches out for help on an urgent and sensitive project, you come.'

'Thanks again, for coming. It was wonderful to meet you and I must declare that this was not how I imagined I'd meet my prince.'

He smiled broadly. 'You need to expect the unexpected. Makes life interesting. You should come to our wedding.'

'What!' Charlotte shrieked. 'Don't tease me. You know you can't invite me like that, and I certainly couldn't explain the invitation to *anyone*. And isn't St George's Chapel already a little crowded?'

'You speak the truth. Sorry. My enthusiasm got a little ahead of me. Anyway, let's get you home.' He signalled to one of his colleagues and together they lifted the stretcher carrying Charlotte. She felt like Queen Cleopatra rather than the substitute princess. They walked carefully through the pine and eucalyptus trees and around the top of Fort Royal. Ten minutes later they arrived at a small clearing where one of the helicopters waited, rotor spinning. Scott clambered inside and helped lift the stretcher. Checks were made that both passengers were firmly secured and noise cancelling headphones were distributed. The rotor began to pick up speed.

'Pinch me,' she mouthed to Scott as the helicopter lifted off the ground. He obliged.

'Ouch.' She slapped him playfully on the knee and lifted herself up for one last look at her rescuers on the island. She waved.

'Bon voyage,' the prince mouthed as the helicopter climbed higher. As the helicopter turned, they could hear an explosion of gunfire below. Scott put his arm protectively around Charlotte and the helicopter suddenly accelerated.

27

JOURNEY HOME

'I'll just be five minutes,' Mason called out to the new driver of the princess's car. He raced along the pier and up the gangplank, startling the second officer.

'You've had a busy night, I hear?' he observed mischievously. Mason hesitated, unsure how to respond.

'You could say that. And now we're in a panic that we'll miss our flight to London.'

'Where's Scott?'

'With Charlotte.'

'She's the damsel in distress?'

'Ahh, yeah. But she's fine now and really wants to get home. So sorry. I can't talk. Gotta get our things and get to the airport. Can you help? She has a rather ridiculous amount of luggage.'

'Women. Of course.' The two men descended to the sleeping quarters, hastily threw maps and clothes into bags and dragged them down the gangplank.

'Thank goodness these monsters have wheels.' The suitcases were noisy on the concrete pier in the quiet of the early morning. The sun was up, and it looked like it was going to be a clear, bright day. 'Where's your Uber?' Mason pointed at the parked car. 'Wow. That's not an Uber?'

'Yep. Can't get anything past you. It's a private car.'

The chauffeur hopped out of the front of the car to load the suitcases into the boot. The second officer's eyebrows raised in disbelief.

'Scott is going to have a bit of explaining to do. When do you think he'll make it back to port?'

'Soon. I know he's on his way.'

'Righto.' And with a quick wave he turned and walked back along the pier to the yacht. Mason sighed. He hoped he'd gotten everything.

The sea looked beautiful as they drove out of Antibes and alongside the pebbled beach. Mason pulled out his phone, took a photo and thought of Miranda. It would be early evening in Brisbane. He punched her number on WhatsApp.

'Hey there. How are you? I'm so sorry I cut you off earlier?'

'That's OK. Where's Charlotte?'

'She's with Scott.'

'She's with Scott or she's *with Scott*?'

Mason smiled and hesitated before replying. 'I think that's a question you should ask her yourself.'

'I've been trying to reach her without success.'

'Her phone battery is probably dead.'

'How's the trip been?'

'Eventful.'

'Did you get what you needed for your story?'

'Too right. Could be career making.'

'So, you won't be coming home any time soon?'

'No plans at this stage. But if things change, I'll let you know.'

'OK.' She couldn't mask the disappointment in her voice. 'Let me know. It's been, what, five years since we last caught up.'

'Something like that. I was just thinking, if this story gets traction, maybe, and it's a long shot, I could pitch to come to Byron Bay and do a special piece on how the story began.'

'That would be awesome. Let me know if there's anything I can do this end to make it happen.'

'Thanks Miranda. That's really nice of you. We're not far from Nice airport now so I'd better hang up. Keep in touch.'

'I will. I promise. Au revoir.' Mason put his phone in his pocket and looked at his watch. 7:35 am. Their plane was departing for Heathrow in fifteen minutes – with or without them.

28

FLYING HIGH

It wasn't possible to talk above the noise of the rotor blades. Charlotte was frustrated. There was so much she wanted to say to Scott. She looked out the window at the wonderful view of the French coastline. Charming houses of orange and yellow. Streets lined with pine trees or palm trees. Yachts bouncing gently on the Mediterranean. It all looked serene, in contrast to the adrenaline-charged way she was feeling. If only she had her phone to take a photo. She signalled to Scott to take a photo. He shot his hand across his neck indicating his phone was dead. He shrugged his shoulders. Moments later they descended and landed gently at Nice airport. A man in white with a wheelchair raced out to greet them. They lifted Charlotte into the chair.

'Ça va. It's OK. Je vais bien. I'm OK. I've got a plane to catch.'

'Yes, you do. But there's been a change of carrier,' Mason called out as he walked towards them with a smile suitable for a toothpaste commercial.

'I thought we'd booked the last flight.'

'Well you know. There's another carrier we weren't

aware of. Anyway, go. The princess is insisting you see her private physician before you go anywhere. This man will take you to him. He's currently inside treating Gilles.'

'Where will you be?'

'Participating in a debrief. You'll need to contribute as well. Go see the doctor and we'll see you shortly.' Charlotte nodded.

'Oui, allons-y merci. Let's go,' she directed the man in white.

The boys watched as Charlotte was wheeled into the building.

'Mate. You've got one heck of a lot of explaining to do.'

'I know. But not now. They're waiting for us inside.

Charlotte was greeted by a nurse, who was also decked out from head to toe in a white uniform.

'Une douche?'

'Yes, I'd love a shower, but I don't have my things with me,'

'Ne vous inquietez pas. We have all you need.' The nurse pushed her wheelchair into an examination room. She then helped Charlotte undress and wheeled her into the bathroom. The hot water felt wonderful and she couldn't help but groan out loud. She was further delighted when the nurse washed her hair leaving a wonderful, lingering scent of vanilla on her skin. After she was dried off a magnificent white terry towelling robe was wrapped around her shoulders. She loved the feel of the fabric against her skin and wondered if she'd be allowed to wear a robe like this on the plane.

'Your things are over here. Choose what you need and

we'll put the rest in a bag for the plane.' The nurse left the room closing the door behind her.

'But these aren't my things,' Charlotte said in wonder as she rifled through the gorgeous garments, toiletries and cosmetics laid out on the dressing room table.

She slipped on a beautiful, deep-blue, bohemian styled, V-neck dress with a wide skirt that would be comfortable for travelling and which would cover her bandage. She brushed her damp hair and spread some of the magical moisturising emollients on her face before applying mascara and lipstick. There was a knock at the door and the doctor walked in, carrying the backpack that she had last seen on the boat before she had slipped overboard.

'My previous patient tells me this is yours.'

Charlotte beamed. 'Yes. That's mine. I must thank Gilles.'

'Perhaps later. Let me look at your injuries.' The doctor examined her leg, reapplied the bandages and checked her vital signs. Satisfied that she'd received good treatment on the island, he called for the nurse.

'Now you must rest this leg and if there is any sign of infection, go and see your own doctor as soon as possible.' Charlotte nodded and the doctor left the room.

'Would you like to have your hair dried before you go?' the nurse asked.

'Pourquoi pas? Why not?'

A call was made and a petite hair stylist arrived moments later. She examined the structure of Charlotte's hair with great interest before attaching the hairdryer to the socket and pulling off one of many brushes from her belt. After different products were applied, another transformation began. Fifteen minutes later a magnificently coiffed Charlotte was wheeled into the debriefing room. If not for the wheelchair, it would have been difficult to recognise the substitute princess. Mason threw his hands in the air.

'I thought you were getting your leg looked at.'

'Tut, tut,' the real princess said as she brushed past the boys to give Charlotte a hug. 'She has a long journey ahead of her and needs to look beautiful for when she is reunited with her family.'

'Shhh. Attention,' Prince Albert directed at his niece. 'Pleased to have you back with us, Miss Wyatt. To recap, Operation Island Sweep was successful and we were delighted to recover you, Scott, Gilles, Gian-Paolo and two of the Sicilian gangsters. We did not however apprehend the man who captured you on the island.'

'You mean the monk?'

'It is highly unlikely that he was a monk. Indeed, he was a wolf disguised as a sheep. What did you learn about him? What were your impressions?' Charlotte looked at Scott and cast her memory back several hours.

'He's a good actor. Very good at playing a monk fishing. We both trusted him. I think he's intelligent. He had anticipated our movements and planned for our capture. He spoke English and French fluently, although I don't believe he was from either England or France.'

'Anything else?'

'He didn't hurt us, and he made it easy for us to be found.'

'I think that was because he wanted to draw attention away from the ransom collection site rather than for humanitarian reasons.'

'And did he succeed?' Charlotte asked.

'Well, yes. He retrieved the bag with the money. But it did not have as much money as he had hoped for.' A small chuckle reverberated around the room. 'We were happy for him to take the bag as there was a tracking device inside. He did however suspect this and dropped the bag into the sea shortly after he was rescued by helicopter and transported to Corsica. We pursued him but were unable to land. He has escaped our net for now. We will pass our information on to the Italian DIA who will continue to look for him. Our job is done'

'Was anyone hurt?'

'Apart from yourself, Gian-Paolo and Gilles, no.'

'And has there been any breech? I mean does anyone know else know about ... everything?'

'We believe that knowledge of the events of the last twelve hours have been contained, and with your help will remain so.'

'You have my word. Our word, in fact,' she added, looking across to Mason and Scott. 'It's not in our interest that this little side excursion is revealed.'

'Thank you for that. Thank you for everything. For agreeing to play a part in my niece's charade. We will always be grateful.' Charlotte smiled and offered her hand to the prince. He shook it warmly with both bands.

'Ready to go home?' Princess Charlotte asked.

'Am I ready? I don't know. I've had such a journey my head is spinning. The only thing I'm sure of is that my mother will be distraught if I'm not back on Tuesday. I suspect she'll be surprised I'm not quite the same daughter who left just over a week ago.'

'Well, nouvelle Charlie. Enjoy your homecoming and keep in touch.' They hugged and Scott wheeled her out to the limousine waiting to drive her and Mason to the private jet sitting on the tarmac. There was a Louis Vuitton travel bag waiting to be loaded into the trunk of the car.

'There are a few things inside to make her comfortable for the trip home,' Princess Charlotte remarked to Mason.

'Oh, just what she needs. More clothes. I'm sure she'll have no trouble paying the excess baggage fees at Heathrow.'

'She'll be fine,' Princess Charlotte said quietly. 'And thank you all again, for everything.' She shook the boys' hands, kissed Charlotte on both cheeks, waved, turned and walked back into the airport building. Scott sighed, put his arm around Mason's shoulder and pretended to give him a tackle.

'So, Scotty. When are you coming to London to finish your captain's exams?'

'Probably in the summer. I'll let you know. Particularly as you owe me a beer or three.'

'Too right I do. Plenty of warning please so I can clear my social calendar.' Scott embraced his friend. Mason looked at Scott and then at Charlotte. 'I'll leave you to help the Princess get into the car.'

Charlotte watched Scott as he walked towards her. He put out his hands inviting her to place her hands in his. She gingerly stood up and teetered forward into his arms. He caught her and pulled her close. Her heart was beating so fast she was sure he could feel it. There were so many things that she wanted to say but for the moment, she remained still in the warmth of his embrace. His arms slipped down her back and she was able to pull her head back past his stubbly cheeks and look into his eyes. They twinkled and he smiled back at her.

'I just wanted to say ...' He leaned in and kissed her gently on the lips. She was taken aback and closed her eyes. She opened them to see him looking at her and regained her composure.

'I just wanted to say thank you for coming to rescue me. Again. A bit unnecessary as I had things under control ...' He kissed her again and this time moved his hands through her beautifully coiffured hair. She lost herself in the moment and returned his kiss. A minute later he released her.

'You'd better go. You've a connection to make.' She nodded reluctantly. He kissed her forehead and opened the car door, helping her to get in. She wound down the window and he leant inside.

'Give my love to your mother. Be selective about what you share with her.' They all laughed as though it was the funniest thing they'd ever heard. 'See you round.' Scott gave a double to tap to the car roof and watched it drive out onto the tarmac.

'Bye bye, Charlie Girl.'

29

FANCY MEETING YOU AGAIN

The hostess poured them both a glass of champagne accompanied by chocolate dipped strawberries as they settled into their seats.

'Not too shabby, Mr Murray.'

'It's OK. Not sure that it's up to the standard of whatever I was sipping at the ball last night.'

'I meant the plane. Not the champagne. And was it only last night?'

'That it was, though it feels as though it was a lifetime ago.'

'Are you comfortable?' They both looked up at a dapper man in uniform standing in front of them.'

'We are, sir. Thank you,' Charlotte replied.

'My name is John Flynn and I'm your captain for this flight. You're travelling today in a Gulfstream G650. A beautiful and very fast bird. We're expecting great flying conditions and we'll have you into London Heathrow in no time at all.'

'No need to rush,' Mason replied as he accepted a top up of his champagne.

'If you need anything, don't hesitate to ask Jean. She's here for your comfort and safety and has already arranged a speedy passage through immigration for you both.'

'That's wonderful. Thank you, Jean.' The hostess smiled and looked at Charlotte.

'Miss Wyatt, if you could give me your ticket and flight details I'll check to see if your flight is on time.' Charlotte pulled out her phone and looked at the dead screen.

'Do you have a charger handy?'

'Of course. One moment.'

Charlotte's phone was connected and burst into life. She gave her flight details to the hostess and started scrolling through her messages.

'Miranda will wonder why I haven't replied.'

'Not so much. I spoke to her a couple of hours ago. Said that you were tied up with her brother.' Charlotte looked incredulously at Mason.

'You said what?'

'I said exactly that. I'll leave it for you to explain *the situation*.'

I don't know what *the situation* is myself.'

'Here. Have some more champagne. This will give you clarity.'

'Let me do that sir,' the hostess chipped in. She took the bottle from Mason and refilled both of their glasses. 'All good for you, ma'am. Your flight is still scheduled to leave on time at 7:55 this evening.'

'Fabulous. Thank you again.'

'Can I get you both something to eat?' They both nodded vigorously, suddenly aware of how hungry they were.

'And did Miranda have any other news?'

'Not so much. We just chatted about this and that.'

'This and that. Sounds interesting.' Charlotte looked at Mason, bemused. 'You do realise she's got a bit of a soft spot for you.'

Mason shook his head and smiled. 'I see. No, I didn't. That's very interesting.' Charlotte laughed. 'You really have embraced that wonderful British characteristic of under-statement. You'll be mocked mercilessly for it when you finally come home.'

'I look forward to that.'

A veritable feast was laid out before them and the friends enjoyed this final leg of their journey together. Captain Flynn was true to his word and the plane landed smoothly at Heathrow seventy-five minutes after it had departed from Nice Airport. A liveried man with a wheelchair met them at the gate and led them into the customs area dedicated to high profile customers. Their luggage was already sitting on a trolley beside a screening machine. Charlotte was surprised to see a familiar face at the immigration desk.

'Miss Wyatt, you return. Tell me. Did you get your story?'

'Indeed, I did. And a lot more to boot.'

'I look forward to reading all about it,' he replied with a mischievous wobble of his moustache as he stamped her passport. 'Have a good trip home.'

'Thank you.'

Charlotte and her luggage were wheeled through to the British Airways First Class Check-in desk.

'No, no. I have an economy class ticket. This is not my queue.'

'Let me check for you ma'am,' the escort offered, taking

her passport and phone. The woman behind the counter smiled broadly.

'Welcome Miss Wyatt. We've been expecting you.' Charlotte looked at Mason who was pulling a funny face.

'You might as well enjoy it. You'll be back in the real world soon enough.'

'Here are your tickets and directions to the first-class lounge. We'll come and get you when it's time to board.'

'Thank you. Can my friend come too?'

'Of course. One moment.' A ticket was printed and given to Mason. Charlotte thanked the escort for his assistance and Mason pushed her wheelchair along to the lounge. It was impressive, but then they were becoming accustomed to impressive.

Once they were comfortably settled in a private nook, Mason selected copies of all the day's newspapers. He was delighted to see Julien's story had been picked up by a few of the news outlets. The articles were small, and on page five, but enough to generate interest.

'I really need to get back to the flat and to write up my piece from the Rose Ball. I also need to shower,' he whispered as he sniffed his clothes.

'If I was you, I'd have a shower here. This will be your last taste of luxury before you go back to the real world and expose yourself to that damp dungeon you call a bathroom.'

'You're so right. Back shortly.'

While Mason was off enjoying the delights of the lounge's bathroom, Charlotte reviewed her messages and calculated the hour in Brisbane. Too early to call but she could send a few messages.

Message to Miranda
Currently chilling at the airport. Looking forward to catching up soon.

Moments later Miranda responded.

Me too. Is Mason with you?

Kind of. He's having a shower.

What? At the airport?

OK. Bit complicated. Hurt my leg. Don't tell Mum. No biggy but scored sympathy + invitation 2 posh lounge. Wangled invite 4 Mason 2. Suggested he take advantage of hygienic environment before returning to squalid flat.

Charlotte waited for a moment before continuing.

Mason tells me you 2 have been texting…

There was a pause before Miranda responded.

Lots to discuss when you get home.

Look forward to it. Go back to sleep. (✿╯‿╰)

Mason returned from the shower a renewed man.
'That'll do me for a couple of days.'
'No need to embrace all the English habits, Mr Murray.'
He smiled, leant over and kissed her on both cheeks.
'It's been amazing. I don't really have the words'

'That's OK. Save the words for your articles. I look forward to reading them.'

'You should have the drafts in your inbox by the time you're back with your family. I'm pretty sure this story has traction.' He paused. 'It's a bit of a pity we can't tell *the other story*. That would have been a *sure thing*, with book deals and movie rights being fiercely contested. Oh well.' Charlotte shrugged her shoulders and smiled at her friend.

'C'est la vie. That's life for you.'

'Have you decided how you're going to explain all this to them?' he said sweeping his arm along her extended leg.

'I'll tell them the truth. I scraped it on a rock.'

'Good luck with that.' He smiled, picked up his bag and looked at her one last time. He shook his head and walked out of the lounge.

Charlotte looked back at her phone and texted her parents.

Just said bye to Mason. Shouldn't be 2 long till I board.
(ᴗ‿ᴗ ❤)

One minute later her parents responded.

Looking forward to having you safely home ❤❤❤ Mum and Dad

Charlotte's mind turned to all the things waiting to be done once she was home. She was due back in class on Wednesday and needed to get the assignment and reflective journal finished. Well no time like the present, she said to herself, as she pulled out her tablet.

Reflective journal

I'm part of a story, like a kindling fire which is already taking hold, there's beauty and romance and mystery igniting interest. A wonderful collection of accelerants for a fabulous story with the power to travel. But who is the person at the heart of the fire and how has she changed from her journey?

Who is she? Who am I?

A student of social media
A sister of a brother I've never met
A daughter of parents desperately afraid of
losing me
An Australian – An Australian abroad.
A traveller. An explorer. An adventurer.
A swimmer. A mermaid.
A model. A muse. A lover of fashion.
A questioner. A dreamer.
A viral sensation?

We shall see.

'Excuse me ma'am?' Charlotte looked up at the agent who had greeted her so warmly at the check-in desk. 'It's time to go home.'

30

ON HOME SOIL

Charlotte arrived in first class with the air of someone familiar with luxury. The flight attendant helped her into her new pyjamas, pulled a blanket over her legs and turned off the light. She was suddenly very sleepy and moments before she drifted off, her thoughts returned to Scott's twinkling eyes and *that kiss*. She was woken twenty minutes prior to landing in Singapore and was wheeled into the first-class lounge. A short rest and an opportunity to practice walking without a limp. Her leg was beginning to feel better.

Upon arriving in Brisbane, she was again taken by wheelchair through a customs area dedicated for special visitors. Her bags were first off the conveyor belt and loaded on to a trolley with a porter waiting for her instructions. She made a special request and he smiled.

She could see her parents behind the rail as she emerged into arrivals. They were surprised to see her sitting on top of her bags on a trolley being pushed by a porter.

'What's all this Purple ...?' her father started, before realising she no longer had long purple tresses. 'What should I call you now?'

'Charlotte is just fine, Dad.'

'You're looking rather glamorous. But princess, just because you look like a movie star doesn't mean you should behave like one. Come down off there.' The porter reached out his arm for support and she gently descended from the trolley

'Ouch,' she cried. 'My foot's gone to sleep.'

Her mother threw her arms around her and held her tight.

'You're home. You're home. Those were the longest ten days of my life.'

Her father ruffled her hair affectionately, tipped the porter and took control of the trolley.

'You've got a bandage on your leg,' her mother stated factually.

'Yep. Fell over against a rock on my last day. Pleased that it wasn't my first day. Would've been terribly inconvenient.'

'I imagine it would have been. I like the new look by the way. Very swanky.'

'Thanks, but I haven't abandoned the gypsy vibe that the previous Charlotte was better known for. I've been experimenting. Isn't that what travel is all about? Being exposed to new situations, trying new things and broadening the mind?'

'Absolutely,' her mother replied before giving her another hug as they approached the car.

'Where'd you get this lovely bag from?' her father asked as he attempted to organise her luggage in the car boot.

'Was a gift from someone I met while modelling at *Paris-Match*. She was lovely.'

'Very generous of her. Must have cost a couple of hundred dollars.'

'Oh, I don't think so, Dad,' Charlotte replied crossing her fingers and hoping he never learnt the real cost of a Louis Vuitton bag.

'So, princess – the essentials. Did you have a good time?'

'Yes.' Charlotte laughed.

'Did you collect enough information for your assignment?'

'Yes.'

'And, did you fall in love?'

Charlotte blushed. 'Maybe.' She could see her parents throw each other a glance.

'How was Mason?' her father asked.

'He's fine. Definitively on the up and up career wise.'

'And Scott?' her mother asked.

'He asked me to give you his love. He's good too. On his way to becoming a captain.'

'How lovely. Do you know when he's next coming home?'

'No. His yacht was in Antibes for a few days for repairs. Next port of call was Portofino, I think. After that, I don't know.'

'And Jacques,' her father enquired, hoping to get his daughter to reveal her secret love. 'How did you find the Frenchman?'

'Charming. Beautiful manners. And such a good kisser.'

'I see,' her father said smiling broadly. 'And shall we expect a visit from Monsieur Jacques at some stage?'

'Who knows?'

'You know, your mother was afraid that you'd meet your English Prince and never come home.'

'That would never happen Mum. I'd always come home – at least some of the time.' They all chuckled.

'Now, I hope you don't mind but your grandfather and Helen have organised a welcome home lunch for you at Byron Bay on Sunday. Just a few people. Get your assignment finished and make sure you're caught up with everything else.'

'Brilliant.'

Miranda was knocking on the door of Charlotte's house at Kangaroo Point in Brisbane ten minutes after they arrived home. Melissa Wyatt opened the door.

'She's in her room unpacking. Can you make sure she doesn't break the wardrobe finding space for her new acquisitions?' They both smiled. 'And lunch is in fifteen minutes.' Miranda tentatively pushed open the door to her friend's bedroom. There were clothes strewn everywhere.

'Yeah. You're home. I want to know everything. Firstly, my oath, is that what I think it is?' she said, examining the Louis Vuitton travel bag.

'Shhh. Dad thinks it only cost a couple of hundred dollars.'

'You didn't buy this? Surely. And why are we whispering?'

'You're right. No need to whisper. No, I didn't buy it. It was a gift from a friend I made at *Paris-Match*.'

'A rather wealthy friend. Did you spend much time with her?' There was a tinge of jealousy in Miranda's voice.

'No. Not too much. Mason and I had morning tea with her before she left to pick up her best friend who was in a spot of bother.' Miranda felt relieved hearing the words *best friend* and missing the *spot of bother*.

'What does she do for a living?'

'Public relations. She managed to get Mason a press pass for the Rose Ball in Monaco. He was so excited. It'll give him the opportunity to deliver something unexpected at work.'

'Tell me about him.' Charlotte shared as many details as she could remember about Mason from the first five days of her trip in London, Paris and Antibes. She mentioned his grotty flat and eclectic flatmates; how protective he was following her mother's request, and his ambitions for becoming a famous journalist.

'And what about when you went to Monaco?'

'We didn't actually spend that much time together. He, for the most part, was off with the paparazzi.' Miranda was satisfied with the answer. She fawned over Charlotte's new clothes and insisted on trying on her new suede boots.

'I think I need to go to London shopping.'

'I believe you. You need to go to London to buy boots.' Charlotte ducked, missing the pillow slung across the room.

With the clothing nearly emptied from her suitcase, Charlotte checked the pockets and discovered her copy of the *Nice-Matin*.

'What d'ya think?'

'You look cute, sailor girl. Not a very good photo of your sailor friend though,' Charlotte looked over her friend's shoulder.

'Curiously, for a man with the confidence of a king, he was notably camera shy.'

'Where's the bottle now?' Charlotte looked in her empty suitcase and was gripped by panic. Mason must have missed the bottle when he packed her bags in haste. It was probably on the boat, unless someone had found it and thrown it away. Argh. No. Where was the boat now? Her joy in making it safely home suddenly evaporated. The bottle was the whole point of the trip. And she hated the thought of revealing she'd lost it; they'd think she was reckless and irresponsible.

'It's on the table, girls,' her mother called from the kitchen.

It was excruciating sitting through lunch. Her parents were so pleased to have her home that neither of them enquired about the bottle. Their questions were focussed on what she saw, what she ate, the clothes she bought and if she'd been cold. The minutia of the questions was expected, overwhelming and adorable in equal measure. Her father noticed she was a little distracted.

'Got jet lag, Princess?'

'Perhaps. A little.'

'I'll be off then,' Miranda offered standing up from the table. Charlotte walked her to the front door and was surprised to see a courier walking up the path.

'Charlotte Wyatt?'

'Yes.'

'Signature please.' Charlotte complied and took receipt of a box. On the back was written OHMS. The bottle was carefully nestled inside bubble wrap. There was a short note written on the back of a beer mat from The Hop Store in Antibes.

Sent securely as requested. Scott

Scott was truly a lifesaver. Not only had he arranged for the bottle to be sent back, but he'd provided an alibi. She could say that this was the plan all along. The OHMS was probably a reference to help he'd received from Princess Charlotte as it was difficult to imagine he could have sent the bottle on a Sunday any other way. She spontaneously hugged Miranda.

'I love your brother.'

'What? Really?' Charlotte caught herself.

'Because. He never stops being a lifesaver. He was so helpful to Mason and I.'

'Is that what you meant? Or is there something else you're not telling me?' Charlotte hesitated and looked at her friend.

'We may have had *a moment.*'

'I see, and ...'

'And nothing. We're oceans apart so it doesn't really matter. It was probably just a 'caught up in the moment' kind of thing. You know. It happens when you're in a different world.' She shrugged her shoulders. 'I should deliver this. See you Sunday. We'll talk more then.' Miranda skipped down the steps and called out as she shut the gate.

'Sunday.'

Melissa Wyatt was lost for words as she looked at the bottle. The anguish and loss she'd felt all those years ago was suddenly present, but it was a different pain. She remembered the loss, the grief, the regret for a life not lived, and the love. She blinked back tears and looked at her husband and then at her beautiful, grown-up daughter.

'We're so lucky to have you. Thank you for bringing this back. Thank you for being in our lives.' Charlotte was taken aback, this was not the level of intimacy, she was accustomed to.

'Really Mum, Dad. Don't be silly. You've been wonderful parents. I'm the lucky one. I know you love me. You let me go when you were afraid and I'm so grateful for that.'

'And we're so pleased you're safely home,' her father gushed, hugging her tightly.

'Enough, enough,' she said laughing. 'I need to finish my assignment.'

Charlotte was about to leave the room when her father asked, 'Why didn't you bring the bottle back yourself?'

'I had an excess baggage problem.'

'Good thinking. And what does the OHMS. on the box mean?'

'Reflects the humour of the sender. Stands for On Her Majesty's Service, you know, like in James Bond. Scott's little joke.'

'What?' her father replied, momentarily taken aback at the reference to Scott.

'Scott sent the bottle. Scott Harmon.'

'Oh yes, of course.'

Charlotte picked up the box and bubble wrap and left her parents alone with the bottle. She'd seen their glances and knew they'd be whispering about her conspiratorial relationship with Scott. That was OK. It was better than them knowing the truth about *everything* that had transpired in the south of France.

Charlotte was excited to see an email from Mason. She'd been so busy since arriving home she'd not checked her messages.

Well Charlotte. We're off and racing. More precisely your story is going wild. I've had such a mad day at work.

Firstly. Julien tells us that your article in the Nice-Matin *has already had 678,980 hits online and he has been inundated with requests for interviews with you and Jacques. Your French sailor has of course set sail and you have flown the coop, so to speak. Everyone is in love with your story and wants to know how it ends. You'll need to decide what you're going to say for the follow-up. Maybe something about what it feels like to come home after such an (insert word here) unforgettable (maybe) experience? Or, if you were open, Hana would love us to write a piece titled, Is it love? You decide. More on what Hana wants shortly.*

I've had sign off from Jane on the following stories.

*'**Loving London: A young Australian's first day**' Tourist perspective*

*'**Jiving in Camden Market**' Shopping special.*

*'**Beauty and the Bottle**' Photos of you looking beautiful in beautiful places.*

*She'd also like to interview your parents with the theme of '**Letting Go**'. You can imagine she'd want them to* *discuss their feelings in letting go of the bottle and then letting go of their daughter, twenty years later...*

Hana has approved the following.

*'**Paris: City of Love.**' I know that's not a very original title, but it suits many of the photos that Jean took last Wednesday at the Eiffel Tower, on the Arc de Triomphe and when we were cruising down the Seine.*

*'**Changing Cities – Changing Styles.**' This one's more a photo shoot comparison highlighting the Gypsy versus the Chanel Charlie.*

*'**Falling in love with France.**' We'll use a selection of pictures of you in Paris and Antibes.*

*'**Is it love? (When a sailor meets a sailor)**' Will be our cover story for Paris Match using that image of Jacques kissing you goodbye on the pier. We're pretty excited about this one. Hana wants to interview you both. Would you be open to reaching out to Jacques to see if he'd be up for it?*

There will be cross promotion between Hello and Paris-Match and we'll all be tracking the hits very closely. We're already fielding enquiries from advertisers about the upcoming issue. We plan to syndicate some of the stories to other news outlets as a way of driving traffic back to our respective home pages.

Oh, and Jane loves my photo of Princess Charlotte and

Dimitri at the palace. It's going to be featured on the next cover of Hello. *So chuffed.*

I know this is a lot to take in. We think that we only have a small timeframe to leverage the interest in your story. That's why we're keen to push hard now.

There are more things I need to chat about, so I'll call you tomorrow night at 7:00pm your time, rather than writing a new version of War and Peace.

Warmly,

Mason

PS How's the jet lag?
PPS No-one believes I got the black eye when I fell over. They say you punched me, discouraging my advances.

Charlotte was overwhelmed. She knew that there would be little chance that her parents, and particularly her mother, would agree to an interview. That was not her problem. She had fulfilled her obligations to *Hello* and *Paris-Match* and anything else was, well, something extra. She'd discuss this with Mason so he was clear.

She opened her assignment and reflective journal to determine what else was needed before she could submit. Her assignment required metrics so she added the website hit rates from the *Nice-Matin* and noted the different articles that would be released shortly. Her reflective journal needed something to bring it together, so she prepared a table summarising her journey.

My journey

About me	Before trip	After trip
Fashion mode	Bohemian/Vintage	Chic/Chanel
Hair style	Long with Purple tips	Short/Serious
Parents attitude	Very protective	Still protective Feeling better about letting go
Communication style	A bit emotive Sometimes speaks without thinking	Calmer More reflective
Status/Identity	Failed student Directionless from career perspective Substitute Child	Will finish fashion degree. Will become online blogger for *Paris-Match* to start my career in fashion. Very loved sister of brother who passed.
Attitude	Unsure. Insecure	More confident Wanting to travel
Options	Bit limited	World is waiting for me

'That'll do,' she whispered to herself. The professor mightn't like it, but c'est la vie – that's life.

31

CHANGE OF DIRECTION

'Come in, Miss Wyatt. Take a seat. Welcome home.' Professor Pete seemed in a particularly chipper mood. 'Had a good trip?'

'You could say that,' she replied understatedly. He leant over and picked up documents from his desk.

'Well done on your assignment. It's good. You make insightful points around the influence of celebrity, beauty and royalty on the potential for a story to go viral. Where'd you get the insights on royalty from?'

'One of my friends got a press pass to the Rose Ball in Monaco, so I tagged along and got a sneak peek at the royal experience.'

'Excellent initiative. Will be interesting to see how the viral metrics progress over the coming weeks. Would you keep a track of them and come back after the Easter break to share them with the class?'

'Sure.'

'Now your reflective journal ...?'

'Yes?'

'Very entertaining but I can't help think that your poetic

writing style is better suited to a creative writing class than digital media.'

'I'm pleased you brought that up, Professor, as I'm considering a change.'

'Oh really? What change?'

'You'll have noticed from my reflective journal that I've fallen in love again with fashion. That's where my passion lies. I'm thinking about going back and finishing my fashion degree.'

'Whoa, whoa. No need to be hasty here. We'd hate to lose you.'

'We?' Charlotte enquired. 'Who's we?'

'The school. The class,' he replied. Charlotte looked at him quizzically. And then the penny dropped, as she realised what his motivations for keeping her in the program might be. Becoming a celebrity would draw attention to Digital Media – the subject, the course and the university. In the same way that *Hello* and *Paris-Match* were using her image to sell magazines and advertising space, the university had an interest in selling courses and programs through successful students.

'Nice to be wanted,' Charlotte offered with a dollop of sarcasm. 'I'll let you know after the break what I decide.'

'Again, talk to me first. I'll make enquiries to see if we can somehow accommodate your passion for fashion within your digital degree.'

Charlotte was thinking about her call with Mason as she arrived home. She knew he'd ask her if she'd spoken to her parents about being interviewed. She'd been avoiding it.

Better get the ugly frog swallowed, as the saying goes, and get the conversation done.

'Hello Princess,' Mason chirped. Charlotte shook her head. 'Hey there. You look awful.'

'Yeah. Thank you for that.'

'Sorry. Thanks for taking a hit for me, physically and reputation wise.'

He laughed. 'It's been worth it. You should see the interest we're getting in your story. Julien tells us that there are now over two million hits to your article in the *Nice-Matin*. As you can imagine, Jane is leaning on me to milk this story for all its worth. Speaking of which ...'

'Yes?'

'Have you spoken to your mum?'

'Ten minutes ago. Her response hasn't changed. She wants this period of notoriety to be behind us.'

'Bother.' Charlotte watched Mason chew his thumb nail. 'I think your period of notoriety is just beginning. What about your French boyfriend? Have you been in touch with him?

'We both know that we didn't have a relationship, although I was happy to run with the illusion to help you sell a few more magazines.'

'But you could pretend ...'

'Mason, you seem to have forgotten that my French friend is as interested in being in front of the media as my mother is. You're flogging a dead horse.'

'Couldn't you at least call him just to check?'

'Alright. Hang on.' Charlotte retrieved Jacque's business

card and called him while Mason watched excitedly. Six rings later. No answer. No voicemail.

'Sorry, Mason. He might be in the middle of the ocean with no reception. Who knows?' Charlotte sat down amused as she watched Mason start chewing his thumb nail again while he considered his options.

'OK. Let's put those interviews to the side for a moment. I've been fielding requests for you to appear on TV chat shows.'

She hesitated. 'I'm not sure ...'

'You'll earn some dosh. If not from the station owner, from *Hello*, who are very keen for your story to keep circulating. Don't you want to travel some more? You'll need cash.' Charlotte suddenly became interested. 'Go on,' she said softly.

Charlotte walked slowly out to the kitchen where her parents were looking at the article in *Nice-Matin* and photos of herself, Jacques and the bottle on the yacht in Antibes.

'Mason tells me that this article has had over two million views already,' she told them.

'Well, you do look rather lovely, *sailor girl*,' her father quipped. She inwardly groaned.

'And you passed on my message?' her mother asked

'That I did. He understands that you're not interested in talking to the media. He's rather tenacious, Mum. I suspect he'll try another angle.'

'Have you been giving him tips on how to wear down my resistance?'

'No, I haven't,' Charlotte laughed, 'so he's shifted the pressure to talk to the press to me. It seems that there are a number of media opportunities he wants me to accept. They'll not only help *Hello* and *Paris-Match* sell magazines, but will generate some income for me. And I'm sure my professor would be delighted. He has already taken a keener than expected interest in my assignment. I'm to give a presentation to class on learning from the trip and the resulting social media metrics after the Easter break.'

'I see,' her father replied cautiously, looking at his wife. There was nothing they could do. Their daughter was an independent adult. How did she grow up so quickly?

32

FIGHTING FOR ATTENTION

Chaotic did not begin to describe his day. Mason spent most of his time on the phone to reporters in France, Germany, Italy, Canada, Singapore, the United States and Australia. When he wasn't on the phone, Jane and Hana were providing hourly updates on *the eyeballs* of each article by geographic and demographic market. The cover photo of Jacques kissing Charlotte had hit the spot and they sold more copies in the first six hours than the previous three editions combined. Everyone wanted to know more. How did the story end? Did Monsieur Jacques and the beautiful Aussie Charlie begin a wonderful romance, or did he simply sail off into the sunset? The likely outcome was hotly debated on Reddit and Twitter. They also loved the story of the Aussie girl's transformation to a sophisticated beauty. Parisians attributed the change to her short immersion in their culture. Pages dedicated to Charlotte's Gypsy look versus Look 2, Audrey Hepburn reborn, began mushrooming on Pinterest. Clothing manufacturers couriered in samples for Charlotte to peruse. *Teen Vogue*, *Instyle* and *Bunte* made enquiries about a cover photo while *Vanity Fair* requested a multi-page spread with an in-depth article. *The View*, a popular chat show in the States offered to fly her in to join their panel discussion.

'We need more, Mason. A lot more. Do what it takes to get the sequel. And quickly. We aren't the only ones who recognise the emotional and economic value of this story.' Jane's emphasis was not lost on Mason. He returned to his desk and stared at his screen. One new email was arriving every thirty seconds and the light on his desk phone was flashing like a lighthouse. He wondered where Scott was. He might be able to help. He sent through a WhatsApp message:

Trying to locate yacht with French sailor who found bottle. Yacht was in your berth in port of Antibes prior to your arrival. Can you investigate for me? Thanks Mate.

His finger started tapping on the desk as he hatched a plan.

33

BACK AT BYRON BAY

The lack of parking spaces on Browning Street was the first indication that her grandparents had invited more than the usual suspects to her welcome home BBQ. Shrieks of delight and the sound of children running could be heard from the backyard. Her cousins must be here.

'She's home. She's here,' her grandfather called out to Helen as he opened the front door and hugged her.

'Welcome home, love.'

'Thanks. And thank you for the investment in my journey. It was a life saver.'

'Any time,' he whispered conspiratorially, 'but don't tell your mother.' Helen arrived and hugged her as well.

'We want to hear all about the trip. Don't leave out a single detail.'

Charlotte raised her eyebrows, looking at her grandfather, and they all laughed.

'What was the best bit?'

Her thoughts flickered back over the trip that already seemed like a lifetime away. She remembered her nerves in arriving at Heathrow, the journey into London on the tube and the easy banter among Mason's flatmates. Then there was the warm welcome at *Hello*, the fish and chips when she was starving, the embarrassment at waking up in Mason's bed. Then there was discovering that the famous song was 'Georgy Girl', not 'Charlie Girl', jiving to the street music at Camden Lock and passing by Big Ben and Trafalgar Square. And the journey continued through the unremarkable Channel tunnel, arriving wearily into Gare du Nord to be robbed, to recover and become empowered and then riding in a police car. There was ice-cream and laughter under the Eiffel Tower before dressing up like a Hollywood star and cruising down the Champs Elysées and the Seine. Then there was that awkward moment with Mason in their Paris hotel, meeting the magnificent Jacques, reading the moving message in the bottle and being lost in his kiss. Such a powerful and mysterious deckhand. And while floating on the memory of this moment, Scott Harmon sailed back into her life allowing her to linger for longer on the French Riviera. The three musketeers then had such fun exploring seaside towns and gorgeous villages. And the next day she met the princess again and received a remarkable invitation to become a Cinderella, a sister, a fiancée, a mother-to-be and a prisoner in one evening. She reflected on the confusion of waking up on the boat, the fear in slipping over the side, the pain in her leg as it hit the rock and the joy of being in Scott's arms. She could still feel the adrenaline as they lay hidden on the island, and later as the helicopter lifted off to the sound of gun fire. And then she remembered trying to say goodbye. She touched her lips, remembering his twinkling eyes and wondered what he was doing today.

'And?' her grandfather asked, 'earth to Charlotte. The best bit?'

'Difficult to say. It was all fabulous. However, I really enjoyed the trip home.'

Her parents beamed. That was the right thing to say.

'And you managed to avoid any trouble?'

'Mostly. Oh, I was robbed …'

'What?' her mother shrieked.

'Mum, I dealt with it. Even got my money back.' Her grandfather hugged her again.

'Miranda is out the back. And we have a surprise visitor for you.'

'Who?' she asked.

'It's a secret.' She looked at her parents, who shrugged their shoulders. They clearly didn't know. Charlotte opened the noisy screen door and scanned the back yard. Her paternal grandfather, Charles Wyatt and his second wife, Lily McDonald, were inspecting the produce in her maternal grandfather's veggie patch. That was to be expected, as the two grandfathers were always trying to outdo each other with the quality of their home-grown vegetables. There were an assortment of her younger cousins playing table tennis. Goodness, it had been years since she'd seen some of them and they'd grown so much they were barely recognisable. Her uncle Miles was super-vising the sausages on the BBQ while chatting with Miranda and a tall woman who looked vaguely familiar.

'You're here. Come over,' Miranda cried out. Charlotte's parents followed her over.

'How's the leg?' the unidentified woman asked. Char-lotte gasped. It was the doctor who had treated her on the island.

'It's good thanks. I received great first aid.'

'Charlotte, you've never met Diane, have you? She's Lily's daughter. She's based in Strasbourg and is a doctor with

Médecins Sans Frontières. Hardly ever gets home but surprised her mother yesterday with a visit between postings.'

'How lovely. And what's it like to work for MSF?'

'Awesome. I get to travel and meet interesting people.' Diane was smiling at her and Charlotte's brain was working overtime. She clearly wasn't the only person with secrets. How intriguing to have a spy backslash doctor in her extended family.

'And is it ever dangerous, the places you visit?'

'Sometimes, but we work in a tight-knit team to make sure we have each other's back.'

'He's here,' Miranda suddenly called out as she rushed around the side of the house. Charlotte's heart leapt. Scott had come home! Unconsciously, she fiddled with her hair. Laughter preceded the arrival of Mason, who was arm in arm with Miranda. She smiled, surprised that she felt pleased and disappointed in equal measure.

'Long time no see, Mr Murray,' she said as she kissed him on both cheeks. 'To what do we owe the pleasure?'

'Jane was concerned that I hadn't been home in a while.'

'Really?' Charlotte replied sarcastically.

'And she thought that if the visit provided me with an opportunity to interview your parents and to escort you to a few chat shows, it would be time well spent.'

'I'm not sure that I trust you to escort her anywhere, Mr Murray,' Melissa quipped. 'I've only just discovered that she was robbed in Paris.'

'That was only because we were momentarily separated. And quite frankly, she proved that she was more than adept at managing herself in a crisis.'

'Sounds like you had quite a trip,' Diane observed with no hint of irony.

'You could say that,' Mason replied, wondering who this woman was. Charlotte wondered if she'd be able to get him away from Miranda to have a private chat. It was not to be. Miranda stuck to Mason like glue, and he didn't seem to mind. She was pleased her friend was happy and surprised that she'd been able to keep his journey home a secret. But then they'd all developed skills in keeping secrets.

A few hours later Mason's phone beeped with an incoming call.

'Hey mate. How are you? Where are you?'

'Near Venice.'

'And you. Where are you? I've been trying to call you for the last twenty-four hours.' Mason said nothing and swung his phone around to Miranda.

'Hey bro. How's things?'

'Ah, so he's gone home. Lucky lad. Are Mum and Dad there?'

'They're coming later. They're at the markets today. I've got someone here who you know.' Charlotte was taken aback as Miranda thrust the camera lens at her. His face was tiny on the phone screen, but his twinkling eyes were unmistakable.

'Hello,' was all she could think to say.

'Hello,' he replied.

'Thanks for arranging the bottle transportation.' They both smiled awkwardly and said nothing. Miranda glanced at Mason, who shrugged his shoulders and turned the phone back to himself.

'Where you headed next?'

'Messina. I might bump into that yacht you asked about. Seems that Monsieur Dessault's yacht has disappeared.

Maybe there's a Bermuda triangle between Rome, Sardinia and Sicily?'

'That'd make a good story.'

'Let me know if you come this way to research it.'

'Unlikely. I've a few stories to follow up here first,' he replied, glancing first at Charlotte and then her mother.

'Too right. Enjoy your time at home. Bye everyone. Bye Charlotte.'

'Who's up for a stroll on the beach?' Mason asked as he popped his phone in his pocket. Miranda raised her hand.

'Me too,' Charlotte quickly added, looping her arm in her friend's. 'We need to talk.'

Melissa Wyatt turned to look at her husband who was helping his brother clean the BBQ. 'You two, right? We're off to the beach.'

'Yep. All good. Enjoy yourself,' Charlotte's father said with a wave. She smiled, turned to Mason and affectionately tussled his hair.

'I understand you want to ask me something.'

Miranda walked arm-in-arm with Charlotte.

'You've been keeping secrets from me.'

'I think I could say the same about you. When did you and Mason get so close?'

'You're to blame. When I couldn't reach you or Scott, I had to reach out to him. And we just kept the conversation going. He told me that he needed an interview with your mum and to get you in front of a few people, so coming home was the best way to convince you. I think his boss was leaning on him but then he's pretty ambitious. I told him about the family get together and that he'd be welcome. You know he's come straight from the airport?'

'Really? Got a job ahead of him if he thinks he can get Mum to talk. We'll see.' They both looked at Mason and Melissa who were deep in conversation six steps in front of them.

When they arrived at the bluff at Main Beach, Melissa and Mason sat down together continuing their conversation. Charlotte and Miranda left them alone and walked down to the sand. Children were playing cricket in the fading light on the shoreline and seagulls were squawking overhead. Charlotte dug her toes into the sand and watched the sand crabs scurry away from the incoming tide. She looked out to Julian Rocks and wondered if any sharks were circling. She thought of Scott and smiled.

After a sprint up to Clarkes Beach and back, Miranda and Charlotte returned to discover Mason sitting on his own on the bluff. He was smiling like the cat who got the cream as they approached.

'I'm guessing she relented and gave into your charm,' Charlotte observed as she playfully flicked him with her baseball cap.

'That she did. On both counts. I not only have her story, but her permission for you to join me on a media tour. She's headed back to the house to get the final signoff from your Dad.'

'Yippee,' Charlotte shouted, bursting into song, 'I'm so excited.'

'Not fair,' said Miranda. 'I wanna come too.'

'It's not a holiday, Miranda. Charlotte is going to be sick of it by the time we get back. I promise you.'

'Can't wait,' Charlotte added wryly immediately downplaying her enthusiasm. Miranda's disappointment at missing out was clear.

'I've an idea,' Mason added. 'While we're away, why don't you plan a break for us all? We could even invite your brother. Somewhere gorgeous where we could surf and soak in a bit of culture. And if we aimed for the end of the year, that would give us all time to save up for the trip. I'm going to need a rest after this. What do ya reckon?' She leant forward and kissed him on the cheek.

'I'm on it.'

Charlotte's father required little convincing. The trip was being funded by money from the photo shoots, and he could already see the confidence his precious daughter had acquired as a result of her recent trip. He was also reassured that Mason would be with her for most of the journey and she wouldn't miss any more study as a result of the mid-semester break. He gave his blessing – as long as she was back before classes restarted.

Later that evening Mason took photos of the Wyatt family with the bottle. The images would accompany an article he planned to write about the bottle's journey home. It was a real shame there was only so much he could share. When the photo session was over, he announced he had something to give Charlotte. The box looked familiar to one she'd taken receipt of last Tuesday. Indeed, inside the box was a bottle with a message inside.

From the other side of the world to you. Can you bring the bottle back when you appear on my show? Ellen

'Yikes,' Charlotte screeched as she passed the message to her mother. 'Have you said yes?'

'What do you think?' Mason replied with a cheesy grin. 'Let me outline your agenda for the next ten days. Tonight, you go home and pack. I'll collect you at nine on the dot tomorrow morning to take you to the *Courier Mail* for your first interview of the day. This will be followed by a photo shoot on the river. Then we'll drive to Ballina, where I've arranged a meeting at the airport with reporters from the *Northern Star* and NBN television. They will inevitably ask the same questions about when the bottle was sent, how you learnt it had been found, the journey to collect it, yadda, yadda, yadda. Then we fly to Sydney and get you to bed early as you are on Sunrise breakfast TV the following morning at 7:00am. There's an interview with a feature writer, Megan Lehmann, from *The Australian Weekend* and lunch with Mia Freedman from *Mamma Mia*. After lunch we'll take a few snaps at Circular Quay of you with *the bottle*. Home for a shower and pack. You have the first spot on The Project at six thirty and then we make a dash to the airport. Lots of time to rest on the flight to Los Angeles. It will be a long night. Wednesday you'll chat with Ellen before we fly to New York for a chat with members of The View on Thursday. We'll also be doing a photo shoot for *Instyle*. Thursday night we fly to London where Jane's very keen to get more photos of you, this time with the bottle. You get Saturday off and we fly to Paris Sunday. Hana has a photo shoot planned on Monday, again with the bottle. I will then say au revoir and leave you in Hana's hands as she accompanies you to Rome for a fashion show. Hana has promised that everyone who is anyone in fashion will be there, so you'll be expected to do some serious schmoozing at the cocktail party. That's it so far. I've booked you out of Rome on Wednesday afternoon leaving you the morning for any emerging opportunities. Does that sound OK?'

'I'm lost for words. However, yes it sounds more than OK. It sounds wonderful.'

'See you at nine tomorrow morning. Sleep well. You're going to need it.'

34

ANOTHER JOURNEY BEGINS

Mason was ten minutes early, but Charlotte was already standing on the veranda with her luggage and nervous parents, eager to begin the second trip. With hugs, kisses and reminders about the importance of frequent communication dispensed, they were on their way.

After the rudimentary elements of the 'bottle story' were explored, the reporter from the *Courier Mail* focussed on her connections to Brisbane, how her family lived in a 'Queenslander,' a quintessential house made of timber with a corrugated iron roof, at Kangaroo Point, and how she studied Digital Marketing at QUT. It was a 'local girl made good' story that would be titled 'Coming Home'. It was a pleasant two-hour drive from Brisbane to Ballina airport where Mason had arranged two more interviews. The reporter from the *Northern Star* focussed on her family's connection to the Northern Rivers region of New South Wales, including her grandparents' community involvement in

Bangalow and Byron Bay and her time as a nipper at the Byron Bay Surf Club. She was nervous when she was asked about how her parents met, a topic she knew little about. However, the reporter soon identified that her mother had been the proverbial girl next door which made her parents' romance, and the story of the bottle's journey, even more intriguing. The interview with the reporter from NBN was focussed on what she'd learnt, and what makes a story go viral. The irony that she was sharing this story on television was not lost on her.

'Celebrity, beautiful locations, a story of love and loss and of course being interviewed on local TV is helpful.' The reporter laughed and wrapped up the interview.

Charlotte loved the flight on the small plane from Ballina to Sydney. They were the only passengers.

'Yes, this is one of the smaller aircraft I use for moving between cities,' Mason offered in an exaggerated English accent.' Charlotte smiled and remembered their last flight together from Nice to Heathrow. Today they were only offered coffee and cheese sandwiches instead of champagne and chocolate dipped strawberries: less posh, more real and equally as fun. Sydney airport was chaotic as it was the end of the Easter holidays, so they didn't get to their hotel until eight. Charlotte opted for room service and trashy television while Mason needed to update Jane and respond to emails.

Their Uber delivered them to Channel Seven's studios at six thirty the following morning, providing time for Charlotte to have her hair styled and makeup accentuated before she sat in front of the glaring lights on set. It was confronting and she regretted the decision to wear a knee-length skirt, as her wound was on display. The 'bottle spot' on the program had only been given two minutes, so there was little time to provide many details of how she learnt about the bottle and the trip to France to collect it. As the interviewer was bringing their chat to a close, she noticed Charlotte's leg.

'You've hurt your leg?' It was more of a statement than a question and Charlotte responded with her first thought.

'Yep. Did it while collecting the bottle. Ran into a rock. Guess it's scuppered any modelling ambitions I may have had.'

'Oh, I doubt that, imperfection is very popular.' And with that they cut to advertisements.

'When did you decide you wanted to be a model?' Mason asked as they walked outside to wait for their ride.

'That would be never. I love fashion and design. Not the same as being a model. I don't know why I blurted that out. It's hard being interesting when you're put on the spot.'

'You do interesting well. Don't worry. Keep it up, we have three more interviews to go.' Charlotte actually enjoyed the interviews with Megan and Mia and noted the interviewers' skill in making her feel at ease. The article in the Australian magazine was to be focused on what it feels like to be immersed in a new country with the title being 'Who's that girl? A search for identity' while the piece in *Mamma Mia* was drawn extensively from Mason's chat with her mother and would be titled, 'Loss, love and looking forward'. Mia reassured her that the story of recovery and of the bottle coming home would provide comfort to many women who had lost children.

Eating fish and chips in the sunshine at Circular Quay while the seagulls squawked overhead was wonderful, and it was fun to watch tourists discovering the beauty of Sydney Harbour, the Opera House and the ferries bobbing at the quayside. After lunch, she and Mason joined the throngs of tourists taking photos from multiple vantage points. People were curious of the girl with the bottle and some recognised her, smiling discreetly or calling out, 'have a good trip.' A few boisterous lads walked past and shouted,

'Don't drop the bottle, love.'

She was instantly reminded of the downside to putting yourself out there in the public eye. They returned to the hotel to shower and pack in preparation for Charlotte's appearance on *The Project*. She was uncharacteristically nervous and fussed over what to wear before slipping on her favourite gypsy shirt, old denim jeans and new suede boots. With confidence restored they caught a taxi to Channel Ten.

'What would you do if someone knocked on your door with a message in a bottle thrown into the ocean many years ago? That was the situation facing our next guest and her family. Please join me in welcoming Charlotte Wyatt to the desk to tell the story of her journey to collect *the bottle*.' A polite round of applause followed.

'So, let me get this right,' Lisa Wilkinson started, 'more than twenty years ago, your brother was born early as the result of a multi-vehicle accident and died a day later. In their grief, your parents wrote him a letter of love which they put in a bottle and threw into the ocean. More than twenty years later it was found by a sailor in France and you've recently been over there to retrieve it. But we all think that there's more to the story than just the collection of the bottle.' Peter Helliar, another member on the panel, raised his eyebrows and the audience laughed.

'I can tell this story in many ways. Yes, it's the story of a bottle that floated from Byron Bay to the south of France. It's also about how a story can make a deep connection and go viral. At a personal level, I could describe the experience of a first trip overseas, of the opportunity to visit new places, to experiment with different identities through fashion and to be exposed to different situations.'

'Let's start by talking about your brother,' Lisa prodded gently, 'what did you know about him?'

'Very little. His name was Scott and he only lived a day, but I've felt his presence all my life. My mother has a photo of him on her desk that was taken at the hospital the day after the accident. They don't talk about him and I can only begin to imagine the pain they felt.'

'We'll put a copy of the letter and the eulogy on our web page for those viewers who are interested, with a warning that you may tear up reading it.'

'Can I ask a question?' Peter intervened.

'Charlotte, did you meet any frogs, err I mean did you eat any frogs?' The studio audience chuckled. Without missing a beat Charlotte responded,

'Oui, et oui.'

'I see,' he replied. 'I picked up a copy of a magazine this morning.' He held up the cover of *Hello* featuring Jacques kissing her at the port in Antibes. The audience cooed with delight.

'Was this one of your new situations?'

'Perhaps,' she replied coyly shrugging her shoulders.

'And are the French men better kisses than the local lads?'

'The locals aren't too shabby.'

'So, there you have it, men of Australia. I think it's time to celebrate and go to a break.'

. . .

They made it to the airport as the final boarding call was broadcast. It was very grounding to be sitting again at the back of the plane. Charlotte smiled. She didn't feel like a phoney here. She fell asleep as the tyres lifted off the tarmac on route to Los Angeles while Mason furiously typed up his notes.

35

CONVERSATION ON THE COUCH

'My next guest has come all the way from Australia. Please welcome Charlotte Wyatt.' Charlotte was momentarily dazzled by the studio lights as she walked out to greet the host of the popular TV show. They hugged and she sat down carefully on the sofa.

'Hi Charlotte. Is this your first time in the US?'

'Yes.'

'First time on TV?'

'Well no. I've been getting a bit of practice in Australia.'

'I see. So why are you here? Oops I forgot. I invited you.' The audience laughed.

'And here's the invitation to prove it,' Charlotte reached into her bag and pulled out the bottle Ellen had sent her. She popped the invitation out of the bottle to show the audience. She then reached into her bag again and pulled out the bottle with her brother's eulogy inside.

'I think this was the bottle you were really interested in.'

'You're right. This bottle has travelled quite a distance,

now on its second journey around the world, starting in Byron Bay, which I see is where your shirt is from.'

'Yes, it's from the Byron Bay Surf Club.'

'Very nice. I'll make sure everyone in the audience gets one.' A loud cheer erupts.

'Where are you and the bottle going next?'

'New York, London, Paris, Rome and then home to Brisbane.'

'Not Byron Bay?'

'Not immediately, but I always get back to Byron Bay. It has a magnificent beach, an earthy vibe, and a family connection that's always pulling me back.'

'So, tell me about what happened more than twenty years ago now ...'

Charlotte explained how lucky she was that the journalist trying to identify the sender of the bottle was a family friend, Mason Murray.

'He's out the back now, and I'd really like him to come out.'

'Of course. Mason, get out here,' Ellen instructed. Moments later a very surprised and clearly delighted Mason shook Ellen's hand and joined Charlotte on the couch.

'The story was outside my usual remit at *Hello*. We focus on fashion, famous people and magnificently styled locations. That the bottle had come from my hometown of Byron Bay sparked my curiosity. I knew Charlotte a little through a friend. Last time I saw her was six years ago when she was being scooped out of the ocean to avoid a school of sharks.'

'What?' Ellen shrieked.

'Stop exaggerating, Mason. Those sharks were a mile away. Australian men are such over-stators.' Ellen's face contorted with shock and the audience shrieked with laughter.

'I think you should listen to your friend, Charlotte. A mile away is kind of close.' She shrugged her shoulders. 'Mason, what exciting things have you been doing with Charlotte since the shark rescue?'

'I've been tagging along while she collected the bottle from a sailor on a super yacht in France and appeared in an assortment of fashion shoots in touristy places, attracting a lot of attention.'

'Did you run into any more sharks?' Mason looked at Charlotte and winked.

'One or two, but Charlotte's pretty good when she gets into a difficult situation.'

'Yes, I've heard that members of the paparazzi can be sharks.' Ellen turned to Charlotte. 'So, what's in the bottle?'

'A letter to my brother, and a eulogy. Mum was in a car accident over twenty years ago. Scott was delivered early and unfortunately he only lived a day.'

'Do you think she'd mind if you read it for us?' Charlotte shook her head and the studio fell silent as she read her mother's message to her brother. The hush in the studio was broken by the sound of plastic tissue packets being opened.

'Wow. That's heartfelt. Thank you. Thank you both and I wish you a safe onward journey.

36

NEW YORK, NEW YORK

It was dark and raining when they arrived late into New York. Charlotte was surprised by the high level of activity at such a late hour and the constant sounds of whistles, speeding taxis and wailing emergency vehicles. She understood why it was called 'The City that doesn't sleep'. She was exhausted. Her head touched the pillow at 3:00am and she didn't move until she heard Mason knocking on her door at 9:00am.

'Sorry Sunshine, I know you're tired. You can sleep in on Saturday. Busy day ahead. We have to be at the studios by 10:00am. I've secured cream-cheese bagels and coffee.' Charlotte opened the door slightly and peeked out at Mason. It was annoying how refreshed he looked. She took the paper bag with the breakfast goods and slunk off to shower.

She liked the women on *The View*. They were bolshy yet sensitive and she soon found herself engaging enthusiastically in the conversation. Like other interviewers, they wanted to know more about the accident and how her parents had dealt with the loss. She responded as best she could and shifted the conversation to the power of *writing it down*, reflecting on the value she had received from keeping a journal for her trip, and what her mother had gained from writing the eulogy.

'How long is your journal?' one of the panel members asked.

'Twenty thousand words, I think.'

'I'd love to read it, particularly the chapter about the French sailor.'

'No one would believe my story. They'd think it was fanciful fiction.'

'Now I really want to read it.' The cries of mirth from the audience were a suitable place to wrap-up the interview.

Mason was slow clapping as she emerged backstage after her appearance.

'You're getting better on the speaker circuit. Another potential career path perhaps?'

'Only if it's a career path where I can sleep in till ten each morning.'

'You did well. I know you're tired. The weekend's not far away and we're off to have lunch and a photo shoot in Central Park with the people from *InStyle*.'

Charlotte stopped and caught her breath as she walked into the park. She'd never seen such an explosion of colour. Spring was on steroids with blossom of pink, purple and creamy hues providing a fairy tale setting. Two small canvas tents were set up near a bridge, with picnic tables laid out with wine, fruit and cheese platters. By now, Charlotte was familiar with the dress-up-drill. Clothes were selected to match the colour of the trees and the texture of the bridge. Her hair was styled with loops and threaded with flowers while her white-face makeup had a distinctive Victorian feel. She was moved through several fashion and setting changes before a final photo shoot in one of the horse-drawn carriages that famously trot along the edge of the park. When the last official shot was taken, Mason asked the photographer to take a photo of them sitting in the carriage on his smartphone. They had fun posing, making victory signs with their fingers.

'I've sent the snap to your parents, Miranda and, I hope you don't mind, Scott.'

'Why?'

'Because he asked me to.'

'I see.'

Reflective Journal - Thursday, 4 April

Sleeeeepy. Can't type properly or keep eyes open.
Trying to keep awake for boarding call after surreal
day. Disappointed I didn't stroll to Times Square,
skip across the Brooklyn Bridge or catch Staten
Island Ferry. Still, did soak in wonder of Central
Park. Must remember I'm here for work. (O⁶‿⁶O✳)

37

ON THE THAMES

Seven hours is too short for a night flight, particularly when one is in need of fourteen hours sleep, Charlotte observed as she rubbed her eyes and made her seat upright in preparation for landing at Heathrow. They took a taxi this time, as the trip was funded by the earnings from Charlotte's photo shoots, and stayed in a hotel not far from *Hello*'s offices at Southbank.

'You're staying too? Not going back to your charming flat?'

'I'm still on protective duty. Can't let your mum down, so I'll need to slum it with you.' The Sea Container was an imposing, modern hotel and they shared adjoining rooms looking out over the River Thames.

'I want to sit here and look at the activity on the water all day.'

'I suspect Jane will have you looking at the water, but not from here. Gotta move on. She's waiting.' Charlotte groaned and reminded herself that she was not on holiday.

'Six million views and climbing, and the article isn't even

in English,' Jane announced as they walked into *Hello's* reception.

'Morning Jane. Lovely to see you too. Yes, we had a good trip thank you.'

'My manners. I'm sorry and I'm so excited. Do you need coffee I think Charlotte does.'

'Yes, that would be lovely,' Charlotte replied, a little overwhelmed.

'Thank you for inviting Mason to join you on stage with Ellen. That was wonderful, and well done you for mentioning *Hello*. Sales have already sparked dramatically in LA, San Francisco, Chicago and New York. And Charlotte, I think you should publish your journal.'

'Err, no.'

'Why not?'

'Because it's private.'

'Well, think about it. And where's that French man of yours?' she said, not pausing for breath between ideas.

'Don't know. He's disappeared.'

'That's inconvenient. Mason?'

'Yes, I'm on it. I've been reaching out for help, but as Charlotte has indicated he's proving rather elusive.'

'Hmmm,' she grunted softly while gently dabbing her index finger on her lips. 'Never mind. Given the popularity of the photos of you on the super yacht with that sailor, we're going to refresh the seafarer's theme and do today's photo shoot on HMS *Belfast*. You'll get a promotion.'

'Pardon?'

'Hana may well have run with you as a sailor in Antibes, well we're going to run with you as captain in London. How does that sound, Captain Wyatt?'

'Aye, aye.'

. . .

They were greeted at HMS *Belfast* by a retired captain who knew the history of the ship and acted as safety supervisor. Charlotte agreed it was a great looking location for a photo shoot, but not always practical with steep stairs and narrow passageways making it difficult for the camera and lighting people to negotiate. Still, everyone remained patient and in good humour, with Jane being delighted with the outcomes. Charlotte's favourite images of the shoot included her sitting in the captain's chair on the bridge looking out across the Thames, undertaking repairs in the engine room with her sleeves rolled up, and holding up the bottle triumphantly on the main deck with Tower Bridge in the background.

The idea of a celebratory dinner somewhere posh had been mooted by Jane with the two Australians but as the day drew to a close, rain started falling steadily and weariness overcame the travellers. It was agreed there would be a celebratory drink only, in the bar on the 12th floor of their hotel.

Jane arrived promptly at 6:00 and ordered champagne. She had a folder under her arm, and pulled out a report to show Mason.

'Look at this.'

'My word,' he said as he turned the pages. 'There've been over ten million hits to the *Nice-Matin* article and both *Paris-Match* and *Hello* have had two additional print runs to meet demand. It will be interesting to see from your contact if there is a spike in weekend sales of *The Australian*.'

'And this is for you.' Charlotte opened the envelope Jane had just given her and gulped. 'We've transferred these funds to your bank account this afternoon and will make another transfer once the expenses from your trip to Paris and Rome have been accounted for.'

'Goodness. Thank you.'

'No. Thank you. It's been a pleasure.'

Jane poured them both champagne and raised her glass. 'May you find your sailor and have a safe journey home.'

Charlotte was conflicted when she woke up at 10:00am the following morning. She loved lying in her huge bed staring out at the river, but recognised that today was totally free of commitments and there was so much in London she wanted to see. A quick text to Mason and plans were made to rendezvous in reception.

With six weeks to go before Harry and Megan's big day, the city was gripped by Royal Wedding fever. Charlotte had a photo taken of herself standing beside a cardboard cut-out of the famous couple outside Buckingham Palace. She smiled at the memory of the nice man she'd met when he released her handcuffs on Ile Sainte Marguerite.

'If you were here in August we could go for a tour of the palace and who knows, you might even bump into Prince Harry.'

'Highly unlikely.'

'Why?'

'Because I don't think he lives here.'

'And you would know this because...?'

'I occasionally read *Paris-Match* and *Hello*.'

'Point won, Miss Wyatt.'

They walked through Green Park where people were sitting in deck chairs enjoying picnic lunches in the early spring sunshine, along Piccadilly where there was a constant stream of red double-decker buses before stopping for lunch at the Wong Kei restaurant in China Town. At

Leicester Square they bought tickets for the four o'clock performance of *The Mousetrap* and then strolled to Covent Garden where they sampled chocolates and Charlotte purchased gifts. After the show they discussed how their trust rating could have been incorporated into the plot. It was a silly discussion. They took a final selfie of the day at Piccadilly Circus and returned to the hotel.

Message to Miranda

Lovely day jiving with your Mason in London. I'm sure he's already told you.
How's planning going for our end of year trip? YOLO
(₀ˋ‿ˊ₀)

Message to Mum and Dad

Getting packed to return to Paris tomorrow.
Trip has been busy and awesome.
Stoked I'm no longer impoverished student.

38

SPRING IN PARIS

Charlotte was pleased they took a plane and taxi to Paris this time. Trains were great but she'd not enjoyed her last arrival into the City of Lights. They checked into the same hotel and Mason chose the day's itinerary, which was to explore Paris by bicycle. On collecting their bikes Mason made sure she turned on her Strava App, just in case they became separated. This happened quite a few times as Charlotte stopped to capture images of buildings and bridges and beautifully manicured dogs, leading immaculately dressed Parisians. Sunday was a popular day to be out in the city and they joined the many other strolling and cycling along the Canal St Martin, before exploring the old city districts of the Marais and Beaubourg.

Hana met them for dinner at seven and wanted to know everything about the trip: who Charlotte had met, what she wore and what questions they'd been asked. She pored over the photos in Central Park, observing the detail in each shot.

'These are good. I'm pleased you're open to something different. We've created a special stage for your shoot tomorrow and the fashion show in Rome will be something quite spectacular. These last two days of your trip will be your most important. Go now. Go to bed. And I will see you bright and early tomorrow morning. Don't forget the bottle.'

Hana had not exaggerated: a beautiful wall of multi-coloured bottles, snaked its way around the stage. It was a work of art and must have taken someone several days to create. The bottles were grouped together in families of azure blue, emerald, caramel, yellow, and cordial red. In one of the bends in the wall was a basic timber table and two wooden chairs. In the next there were buckets full of different coloured tulips, and in the final setting a chaise lounge covered in an intricate Jacquard brocade. Jean, Clarice and Mireille were again on hand to transform her from casual Charlie to scintillating Charlotte. She was dressed in ballgowns with metres of chiffon in light pink, mushroom and grey.

For the first arrangement she sat on the chair looking at the bottle in the middle of the table. Jean had created a distinctly sad ambiance of waiting for someone to come home, as depicted by the empty second chair. In the second scene, Charlotte pretended to water the plants from the bottle and in the third she reclined in the lounge while a heavenly light from above shone down on her. They were certainly artistic, but Charlotte felt that they'd gone too far in using the bottle and projecting meaning from its image. While this was the way that high end couture was some-times marketed, she decided this would be the last time she would pose with the bottle.

Monday evening was time to say goodbye to Mason. He was

flying back to London while Hana and Charlotte were headed east to Rome. It was sad to say goodbye and they held each other tight.

'No more surprises please. Don't get caught up in *anything*.'

'I'll do my best.'

'Hana will look after you. Sounds like it'll be quite a show. You should be able to make some useful connections.'

'You're always on the make, aren't you, Mr Murray?'

'You've got to seize the opportunities where they present themselves.'

'Alright, I will. And don't forget your surfing break idea for the end of the year. Don't want to let Miranda down.'

'Try and keep me away.'

39

ROME IS FALLING

Charlotte joined fifteen other models reporting for makeup at eight the following morning. There was a buzz of excitement in the room, with many transfixed by the beauty of the location. The fashion show was themed Eastern Surprise and was a fusion of traditional Mongolian and Japanese clothing with a modern twist. It was being held at the St Regis Hotel in Rome. The ballroom had been transformed, with a long walkway and orchestral area. The clothing included traditional costumes reimagined with bold coloured taffetas and silks. Each model had their hair rolled up at the back in a series of buns while their face, neck and collar bones were expertly painted in a rainbow of geometric stripes or patterns. Charlotte loved listening to the chatter of the models in their different languages as they lined up to go on stage: vous êtes belle; você é linda; bellissima; brava chiquita. She was thinking about the last words she heard as she made her entrance into the crowded ballroom and faced an explosion of lightbulbs.

She kept her expression neutral, as instructed, and scanned the room for Hana. It surprised her to see her chaperone near the end of the runway, and in the front row, engaged in animated conversation with Princess Charlotte. Of course they knew each other – she'd met the princess at *Paris-Match*. Hana spotted her and raised her champagne glass while the princess smiled, ever so slightly, and winked. It took self-control not to smile back. It appeared that Hana had already enjoyed several glasses of champagne. Perhaps she was celebrating the success of *her* little Australian. She looked to her right at the end of the runway, straight ahead, to her left and then straight ahead again. It was at this moment that she spotted several men in white uniforms standing at the back of the room. They were a handsome collective and Scott Harmon was unmistakable among them. Charlotte looked directly at him, but he didn't recognise her. Then again, her mother would have had difficulty with the kaleidoscope of colours splashed across her face. She turned, walked back to the middle of the runway and paused again. All eyes were on her as she prepared to turn for the final walk to the change room. As she turned slowly, she noticed a man she thought she knew. Perhaps he was a member of the paparazzi who'd attended the ball in Monaco? Surprisingly, he was not looking at the models on the runway. Instead, he was staring at Princess Charlotte. A creeping fear engulfed her as she entered the change room for her final outfit. Two dressers quickly removed her dress and touched up her makeup before helping her into her kimono. With ten seconds left before she hit the runway, she furiously typed: *Monk is here*; send.

She hoped the princess and Scott would know what to do.

She was relieved to reach the midpoint of the runway and see an empty chair beside Hana. Hana looked up, smiled and signalled for the waiter to top up her champagne. The princess had made it out. Charlotte turned, walked to the end of the catwalk to see that Scott had moved closer and was looking directly at her. In time to the music she made a dramatic gesture of pointing to the right and then swinging round to point to where she had last seen *The Monk*. He was gone. She then returned to the front and shrugged her shoulders. The audience laughed at this unexpected piece of theatre. There was a shout at the entrance and Charlotte looked up to see a number of Carabinieri flooding into the room. Scott saw this too and immediately jumped onto the stage and scooped her up in his arms. The audience was delighted, thinking this was part of the show and the conductor changed the music to 'Up Where We Belong'. Scott jumped down from the stage, still carrying Charlotte, and the crowd slowly parted for him to walk out unobstructed. The other models emerged onto the catwalk cheering and clapping with delight, while waiters moved among the crowd topping up their drinks.

Once they were outside the ballroom, Charlotte suggested that Scott put her down.

'I think it's safe now.'

'We don't know where he is. Let's get to somewhere more secure.'

'I'm meant to stay and network.'

'Nope. Not today. Too risky.' He accompanied her back to the dressing room where her kimono was returned to the rack and the makeup wiped from her face. She checked her phone and was delighted to see a message from the

Princess checking to see if she was safe. *All good here,* she texted back.

They caught a taxi back to her hotel, with Scott checking the room before he'd let her enter.

'You know Scott, he was looking for the real Princess not me. And if he suspected that he'd kidnapped the substitute, he certainly wouldn't have recognised me under all that makeup.'

'Maybe. But the man is clearly audacious, monied and well connected. Who knows where he might turn up next?'

'You do realise that you were the substitute tonight? Anyone who knew that I was *the bottle* girl, may think that you were my French sailor Jack Dee. Goodness, Jane and Hana would love that.'

'I don't think that anyone was paying attention to me. You know, you were so beautiful on the runway, I was transfixed. I ... I didn't recognise you.'

Charlotte sighed. 'If only you'd stopped at the *I was transfixed.*'

'I didn't mean that. You know I didn't mean that. You're just so surprising and adventurous and ...'

'I could say the same about you, Mr Officer and a Gentleman.'

'Sorry about that. It was the only thing I could think of. You certainly couldn't run in that Japanese dressing gown. I hope I didn't embarrass you.'

'Au contraire. It was the perfect ending to my modelling career.'

'Ending?'

'Yes. Today was my last day. I fly home tomorrow and resume my rather ordinary life as a student.'

'I don't for a moment imagine your life will ever be ordinary.' Charlotte looked at Scott and slowly smiled.

'What prompted you to come to the fashion show today?'

'The consortium who own the yacht I'm working on have an interest in a luxury goods company. There were a few free tickets going and I wondered if you might be there. Wasn't hard to convince a few of the team to tag along.'

'That was a bit of a shot in the dark wasn't it? How'd you know I was in Rome?'

'Mason may have brought it to my attention.' She smiled and wasn't sure how to respond.

'I don't know about you, but I'm starving.'

'Why don't we eat in? You have a lovely terrace.'

'Because I haven't seen any of the city. Last night we had fittings and briefing on how to walk and how not to smile and this morning we had to arrive early for makeup. I can't be in Rome and not have a Roman Holiday.'

Scott regarded her thoughtfully. 'It is a wonderful city and the monk is probably miles away now, but you must stick close to me. To be sure.'

'If you insist.'

It was a short walk to the grand Piazza Navona where there were flower boxes and fountains with eclectic statues. Musicians and painters displayed their art for the pleasure of tourists and locals alike. They took a table in the sunshine and soaked in the party atmosphere. The enjoyed bruschetta with tomatoes, Parma ham, buffalo mozzarella, gorgonzola and walnuts followed by carbonara rigatoni. Elderly Italian couples looked at them and smiled. Scott took her hand and led her through narrow lanes to the Spanish Steps and the Trevi Fountain, where she threw a coin, like thousands before her, in the hope of returning soon. Scott rented a Vespa and drove past the Pantheon and Coliseum and up to Palatine Hill where they ate gelatos while taking in the view. It felt dangerous weaving in and out of the traffic, but she loved the thrill of the ride and having her arms around Scott.

Scott picked up a bottle of Montepulciano on the way back to her hotel and they sat on her terrace listening to the sounds of the day; scooters honking, tourist chatting animatedly and children chasing balls in the narrow alley-ways. A gentle knock on her door startled them. Charlotte walked slowly to the door with Scott close behind, sending hand signals that she was not to open it.

'Si?'

'Just checking you're OK, Charlotte.'

'Oui, oui, yes I'm fine Hana.' Silence for a moment. 'You were beautiful today. You were perfect, cherie. Let's talk about it over breakfast. Ça va?'

'Oui. Ça va. Tomorrow.'

'Dors bien. Sleep well.'

'You too, Hana.' They both stood motionless, listening to Hana's departing steps and the opening and closing of the door to the adjacent room.

'She knows you're with me.'

'Does that matter?' he asked. Charlotte shook her head as she regarded his dark eyelashes and smiling eyes.

'I think ...' he started before being interrupted by his phone. He answered it while still looking at her. He finished the call. 'I need to go back to the yacht. We're leaving tomorrow and I need to get provisions. Will you promise me you won't leave the hotel without Hana?'

'I will.'

'And will you keep out of trouble?'

'That, I can't promise.'

'I'd expect nothing less,' he said, laughing. He leant forward and kissed her gently. Charlotte closed her eyes and savoured the moment, leaning in to him. He pulled away a little and put his hand in his pocket. 'Here's my card with contact details. Be nice to keep in touch.' Charlotte regarded the card carefully, wondering what *nice to keep in touch* meant. And then he was gone. She double locked the door and went out to the terrace to retrieve the wine glasses. He was at the end of the lane. He turned around and smiled and then disappeared around the corner.

Hana gave her a conspiratorial smile as she joined her at breakfast. Charlotte didn't want to talk about Scott, her best friend's brother, frequent rescuer and occasional kisser.

'Sorry I skipped out on the networking.'

'You don't need to apologise, darling. With such a dramatic exit you guaranteed that *everyone* was talking about you and your Jack.'

'That wasn't Jacques.'

'Shhh. Don't tell anybody. It was PR gold. Have you seen Twitter this morning? #JackisBack is trending as well as #journorequest as reporters seek to interview you. Charlotte looked at Twitter. There were photos of Scott scooping her off the stage from multiple angles, with images of a delighted audience capturing the moment on hundreds of smartphones.

'It's a pity you didn't get the opportunity to meet Princess Charlotte. Absolutely delightful girl. Loved everything you were wearing. I guess it was easy for her to imagine wearing those clothes as you share the same build, facial structure, eye colour and ...' Hana stopped talking and observed her closely. She shook her head, dismissing whatever idea was there and continued. 'We should take a taxi together. I fly out an hour before you and there is wonderful shopping at the airport.'

Hana held her tightly as they said goodbye at the departure lounge.

'Bonne chance cherie, and keep in touch.' There were three kisses and she was off. Once Hana was out of sight, Charlotte returned to her gate and took a seat just as Mason called.

'Where are you? Have you seen Twitter?'

'I'm at the airport on my way home and yes, I've seen Twitter.'

'You know that wasn't Jack? It was Scott.'

'Well d'uh. Don't tell anyone.'

'That's what Hana said.'

'Jane's thinking about investing in billboard advertising, using one of the images from the show, if that would be OK with you.'

'To be honest, Mason, I'm over being a celebrity.'

'Well, think about it on the way home. Don't close off your options too quickly.'

'Sure, Mason,' Charlotte sighed. She knew there was little point in discussing this now with her tenacious friend.

'Great. I'll be in touch soon. Bon voyage. Love to your parents, and give Miranda a hug from me.'

Message to Miranda

Fabulous trip. Mason sends you a big hug.
Bumped into Scott at a fashion show. So much to tell.
(◕‿◕✿)

Message to Mum and Dad

Busy last day in Rome. At the airport now. Home soon.

EPILOGUE

Charlotte slipped her purchases into her Louis Vuitton carry-on luggage and picked up a copy of the international edition *of The New York Times* while waiting for her flight to be called. News about the upcoming marriage of Meghan Markle to Harry Windsor was still making front page news. She thought about the prince, Scott, Mason and the elusive Jacques Dessault. She realised she should give Jacques notice about the 'fake news' circulating about his presence at a fashion show in Rome. She dialled his number and was startled when someone answered immediately.

'Yes.'

'May I speak to Jacques, please?'

'Who is this?'

'Charlotte Wyatt.'

'And what is your relationship with Jacques?' Charlotte hesitated. What was her relationship with the illusive Frenchman?'

'We're friends.'

'I'm afraid he's tied up at the moment.' The phone rang off.

Shaken, Charlotte sat down and absentmindedly flicked through the rest of the paper. On page six there was a small article about a missing industrialist.

The family Dessault has launched a private missing persons investigation and are offering a reward for information related to the whereabouts of Jacques Dessault. The last time he was seen was on the super yacht Taormina Triumph, in the port of Antibes on 22 March, 2018.

SONG REFERENCES

The Seekers. 'Hey there Georgy Girl', Lyricist: Jim Dale. Composer(s): Tom Springfield. 1966. Album, *Come the Day*.

Mancini, Henry, Instrumental theme from the Pink Panther, 1963.

Denver, John. 'Leaving on a Jet Plane', 1969. Album, *Rhymes and Reasons*.

Mancini, Henry. 'Moon River' Theme song from Breakfast at Tiffany's, Composer: Henry Mancini. Lyricist: Johnny Mercer. 1960

Composer: Coleman, Cy & Lyricist: Fields, Dorothy. 'If My Friends Could See Me Now', 1965. Made famous by Sammy Davis Junior

THANKS FOR READING

I hope you enjoyed reading *Substitute Child*. Great to learn what you thought if you have the time to pen me a few lines, and, if you feel so inspired, a review online would be appreciated. You can email me at janeellyson@gmail.com and I'm also on twitter @janeellyson1 – if you're a tweeter and on Pinterest at https://www.pinterest.com.au/janeellyson/boards/ – if you're a pinner.

I'm currently writing the sequel to *Substitute Child* called *Roman Roulette*. It is a thriller set off the Italian coast with Charlotte once again having to use all her skills to extricate herself from a dangerous situation. If you are on my mailing list, you will receive advance notice of its publication. You can sign up for my newsletter at www.substitutechild.net

Happy reading,

Best, Jane

Twitter @janeellyson1

WALKING TOUR OF ANTIBES

1. Start at the Ferris wheel beside the port of Antibes on Avenue De Verdun.

2. Walk alongside the ramparts (old walls) of Antibes down to the far end of the port. There will be hundreds of leisure craft gently bobbing in the water.

3. Walk back towards the wall and under the archway taking the left turn up Av. de la Salis. You will enjoy the same wonderful views back to the port and across La Gravette Beach that Jacques showed Charlotte.

4. Continue along this road for another twenty metres and enjoy looking over to the Cap d'Antibes.

5. After fifty metres stop at the Picasso museum and then wind your way through the narrow streets back to Cours Masséna.

6. I recommend you stop at the Antibes Provencal Markets to take in the smell of flowers and spices.

7. Then follow Rue Sade down the hill until you emerge into a large town square. I recommend you, pick up a gelato and then enter Rue Thuret.

8. Follow Rue Thuret until the end where it joins Boulevard d'Aguillon. Turn right and you will be a few steps away from the Hop Store, where Charlotte, Mason and Scott enjoyed their first drink together. (Let me know if the sign, *No kissing in the bar unless with staff,* is still there).

WALKING TOUR OF CANNES

1. Start at the Palais des Festival et des Congres at the end of the Croisette. Look at the hundreds of hand-prints of movie stars who've left their mark while visiting the city.

2. Walk along the Croisette taking in the sparkling Mediterranean on your right and the stunning hotels on your left. You could walk a long way here taking in the wonderful seaside ambiance. I propose you cross the road and take Rue Mace up to Rue D'Antibes. The shops may tempt you, but I suggest continuing up Rue Chabaud until you come to the pedestrianised street of Rue Hoche. You will see a number of lovely cafes on this street.

3. Continue along Rue Hoche until you reach Rue de 24 Août and turn left and walk back down to Rue d'Antibes.

4. Turn right and walk a few hundred meters down

this shopping street then turn right at Rue Louis Blanc. Walk three blocks and you will see the Marche Forville on your left.

5. Walk through to the end of the market and turn left at Rue du Docteur Pierre Gazagnaire, walking down to Rue Felix Faure which joins Rue Georges Clemenceau. Turn right here. Take Rue du Barri to walk up to the castle to view the city of Cannes and Îles de Lérins.

6. When you walk back down the hill the same way, walk across Rue Georges Clemenceau and down to Quai Saint-Pierre. You can walk along the waterfront, to the large carpark where you can take a boat out to Îles de Lérins. I would suggest you visit Ile Sainte Marguerite if you are pressed for time. You'll not only be able to visit the forest where Scott and Charlotte were held captive, but also the cell which was home to the 'Man in the Iron Mask'.

ABOUT JANE ELLYSON

Jane has a deep connection to the Far North Coast of New South Wales and also to the south of France. Her great grandparents owned a farm a little way out of Byron Bay before moving into a house on Browning Street. Her grandparents were long term residents of the nearby town of Mullumbimby. Jane currently lives at Possum Creek, not far out of Bangalow – or she would if she was real rather than being the pen name of someone who would prefer to remain anonymous. This is her second novel. Her first novel was *Over Byron Bay*.

READ OVER BYRON BAY

Read Charlotte's parent's story in 'Over Byron Bay'.

Melissa Bourne and Andrew Wyatt were neighbours in the country town of Bangalow in Australia. Friends, good friends were all they'd ever been. This situation suited them both until Andrew found someone else. Surprised at her jealousy and with an international job offer in hand, Melissa left the country. She accepted a job offer in Boston, met Jonathan Brinkley, married and settled into life in the U.S.

Five years later she returns to Bangalow for a visit with her father, shortly after the death of Andrew's mother. The two meet briefly at the funeral, and the day before she flies back to Boston providing an opportunity to rekindle their relationship and to recognise that their feelings for each other go beyond friendship. Melissa returns to the States in turmoil.

Over Byron Bay is a story of friendship. A deep friendship that neither Melissa nor Andrew were prepared to risk for love.

It's a story of heartbreak and hope. Of two people with extraordinarily bad timing.

It's a story or relationships within and between families.

It's a turbulent story of running away and of new beginnings set between Bangalow, Boston, Brisbane and Byron Bay.